Praise for *To Lay to Rest*

"… reminds us of the power of a well-delivered narrative…. Summie's stories emphasize [our] shared humanity, and there is something accessible, recognizable and timely for everyone."—*The Vail Daily*

"This debut collection works together to form a Cubist portrait of grief….Summie's ghosts linger."—*The Minneapolis Star Tribune*

"The universal issues and dilemmas at the heart of Summie's stories and her focus on families give *To Lay to Rest Our Ghosts* wide appeal. You'll want to talk about these characters as if you knew them, and you'll want to revisit these stories more than once."—*BethFish Reads*

"…will resonate with readers who themselves may have experienced these life-changing family moments that seem small but are really huge."—*The St. Paul Pioneer Press*

"The stories center on the complexity of family relationships with such empathy and humanity that novelist Steve Yarbrough called the book "nothing short of magnificent."…her elegant prose shines in this collection."—*Chapter16.org (also appeared in The Knoxville News-Sentinel)*

"…a beautifully crafted work of art…"—*Centered on Books*

"…impressive…."—*Largehearted Boy*

"…the stories in this collection are some of the most beautifully written I've ever read ….in many short story collections not every story resonates with me, but in *To Lay To Rest Our Ghosts*, they all did."—*Bookstalker Blog*

"There are lots of story collections with a very strong connection to place. There are also lots of collections with great range in their locales....*To Lay to Rest Our Ghosts* is a wonderful achievement because it meets both of those goals. I found myself attached to each story and its places—carefully enhanced by characters whose lives and thoughts and situations are quite easy to feel connected to."
—Hans Weyandt, Milkweed Editions Bookstore

"Caitlin Hamilton Summie is an author in full flower. These ten stories embody craft, care, an obvious love of language, and a deeply generous understanding of people and places. *To Lay to Rest Our Ghosts* is a completely pleasurable read."
—Joni Rodgers, NYT bestselling author of *Sugarland*

"...*To Lay to Rest Our Ghosts* is nothing short of magnificent. The author's sense of place is extraordinary, and it informs every word she writes. Her characters are as real as anybody you know in the town where you live, and their lives are depicted with quiet dignity. The stories are both intense and economical. I've gotten very hard to please, but I loved this book."
—Steve Yarbrough, author of *The Realm of Last Chances*

"Beautifully crafted, Caitlin Hamilton Summie's short story collection is a lyrical elegy about loss and love, family and home. Her writing reminds me of the grace and sensitivity found in stories by Ann Beattie and Elizabeth Strout. I can't wait to introduce *To Lay To Rest Our Ghosts* to Gramercy Books customers!"
—Linda Kass, Owner, Gramercy Books and author of *Tasa's Song*

To Lay To Rest Our Ghosts

"Tags" originally appeared in slightly different form in the *Beloit Fiction Journal*
"Points of Exchange" originally appeared in slightly different form in *Puerto del Sol*
"Fish Eyes in Moonlight" originally appeared in slightly different form in *Wisconsin Review*
"Sons" originally appeared in *The Mud Season Review*
"Brothers" was previously available in the *Emerging Writers Network Holiday Gift Email, 2016*
"Geographies of the Heart" originally appeared in *Long Story, Short*
"Taking Root" originally appeared in *Belmont Story Review*
"Growing Up Cold" originally appeared in *Hypertext Magazine*

ISBN-13: 978-1-944388-06-5
Library of Congress Control Number: 2017934561

Fomite
58 Peru Street
Burlington, VT 05401
www.fomitepress.com

Cover art: Snow Storm, John La Farge (1865)

For my family

Contents

TAGS

JIMMY WESTON HAD his Dad's dog tags. He wore them around his neck on a steel chain and had this funny habit of rubbing them back and forth between his fingers. We'd be playing marbles or collecting tin for the war effort; we'd be jumping on cracks to break Hitler's back or be waiting, just waiting, for the whole thing to end, and Jimmy would talk and rub those dog tags together, and I'd listen. That's mostly how I remember those days: Jimmy and me sitting on the curb, tired of marbles, tired of tin, him with that sound of his father, and me with nothing of mine but his name.

My father enlisted when I was four. He was quiet about it, according to my mother, but she knew he was planning on signing up. Before the war, the men met after their day shifts for a beer or a game of ball or cards, but not after the war began.

Then they started home when the whistle blew. Too sick of the brewery to think of beer, too distracted to finish a game, they peeled off from one another at each doorway with cat calls and jokes and day weary voices. But then the talk began.

THE SKY WOULD go pitch, lights would fill window frames, and then the men would come over. Jimmy's Dad and my uncles and others my mother does not name. She'd be standing at the sink, hands greasy and dripping and slick, and there would be a soft rap on the door, or the low groan of the wooden porch steps, or just the feeling, suddenly, that she was not alone, and she'd turn, and there was Uncle Joey, or Uncle Ray, or any of them.

"How many?" I once asked. I was fifteen, maybe sixteen, wanting to hear the details again, confident in my newly discovered remove.

She shrugged. "Five," she said, "six, sometimes seven. All around that little kitchen table."

"How come they came to our house?"

She shook her head. "We were the mid-point, half way down the block. I don't know. Maybe I served the best coffee." She smiled, but her smile quickly faded.

"They knew," my mother said, "that they wouldn't all come back. We all knew that."

I nodded, but only as a reflex because we did not all know that. I didn't. Jimmy didn't. We were the littlest ones, the ones who learned slowly, much later than everyone else, what the absences meant. I remember catching on. I remember sitting on the curb late one afternoon in the middle of winter, wrapped in wool, listening to Jimmy rub those dog tags together. I remember thinking, as the sun went down and the chill set into me, that Jimmy's father was up there somewhere, in bits and pieces.

JIMMY WESTON AND I got to be friends playing marbles. I was sitting on the sidewalk outside the house one day, placing my marbles along the cracks in the pavement in neat rows of blue and yellow and green. My favorite marble was a solid red, the only red one I had, and it was my shooter. The day was quiet, a Saturday, or maybe even a Sunday, and cool. I wore a plaid hand-me-down jacket from my cousin, Linda, and my cousin Larry's old baseball cap. I was the youngest and got whatever old clothes fit.

I didn't like Jimmy much. Jimmy had pale skin and freckles and a soft voice that was sometimes hard to hear. We were the same age, younger than most kids in the neighborhood, but we didn't spend much time together then. Every time I asked him to play, he had a cold or the flu or a sore tooth or his left toe was throbbing. I stopped asking. I played by myself or with two boys down the street, Tommy Ocerly and John Swenson, but Tommy and John were best friends, and I was an awkward addition.

3

That day I sat on the curb and admired my marbles. I had twenty-one in swirling colors, and I loved to watch the colors as the marbles shot across the pavement. I was used to being alone, and I'd started talking to myself, using a voice like the ones I heard on the radio, talking in the same clipped manner. I started to describe my marbles, imagining the marble tournament of the world, imagining a final match between me and a nip maybe.

"You talking to yourself, Dolores?"

I looked up quickly, and coming across the street with a small cloth bag gripped in one hand was Jimmy Weston, limping. I shook my head at his limp, but he misunderstood.

"Then you must be talking to me," he said, and stepping in a hop over the curb and up onto the sidewalk, he knelt down. He let his marbles out onto the pavement slowly, holding them in with his hand and forearm. He looked me in the eye. "I'll play you for the red one," he said.

ALL THE MEN in my family went, first Dad in '42, then Uncle Ray, then Uncle Joey, and so on, until all five were away in Europe. They disappeared quickly, I guess, though one by one, and then the women pulled together. This is what they tell me, my mother and my aunts and my cousins: Grammy picked up the phone after the last man had gone and called my mother; and my mother called her sister, and that was that.

Five women and their children moved into Grammy's once spacious and echo-y house in Kansas City, and waited for their men to come home. For my mother and me, the move was minor, only one block down.

I knew the men in my family by photograph, but the only photograph I studied was my father's. I'd sneak into the room my mother shared with my aunt, and I'd stare at the photograph of my Dad on her dresser. I'd look at the ridge in his nose, the little bump part way down, and I'd rub my nose, which was smooth and long. Yet the minute I closed my eyes and tried to remember his face, I saw nothing. On a good day, I remembered the smell of soap when he hugged me, the smell of cigarettes in his clothes and hair. On a good day, I remembered his voice saying my name.

"Does he like pancakes?" I asked one morning as I watched my mother flip a pancake in the griddle.

"Yes," she said, "he does."

"Does he like sausage?"

"That's his favorite."

"Does he like milk?"

"No, he likes beer," Larry said. Larry, who had both arms on the table, which I was not allowed to do. Larry, whose hair was white, not blond or flaxen, but white. The high school girls loved his hair. They loved his face. I was small, and even I knew this. I loved his hair. I loved his face.

My mother turned and scowled at Larry. Her hair was auburn then, and her cheeks that morning were flushed red. "He also likes milk, Lawrence."

"Lawrence!" I cooed.

She turned back to the griddle, and Larry tapped me on the arm. He rolled his eyes. He stuck his fork into one of my pancakes and lifted it off my plate.

My mother tells me about what her days were like, about the long wait for the mail in the mornings, when whatever women had the day off clustered around the kitchen table, sipped coffee, waited. Just bills today. Just a circular. They bought seeds and planted a victory garden, over which Grammy presided in khaki pants and a straw sun hat, and which my mother weeded regularly. They grew carrots and lettuce and tomatoes. They used their ration books and bemoaned the day cheese went on the point system. They tore up old curtains and sewed play outfits for me, made dish rags from the rest. And they waited, dreading the appearance of the uniformed telegram company man, watching as he walked down the street, praying to themselves that he'd pass the house.

My mother tells me these things in bits and pieces. She's old now, and the older she grows, the more romanticized the war era becomes. "All of us in that one house, making do," she'll say. "Not like today." No, not like today, when I live across the city with my husband and she still occupies Grammy's cavernous old house by herself.

"You know," my mother tells me, over and over, "your dad always wanted to be a pilot."

"Yes," I reply, uncertain what I am affirming, that yes, he wanted to fly, or yes, she's told me. The repetition is oddly comforting. It is the unexpected reminder that upsets the delicate balance, allows grief an entry, gives life to a sadness long laid to rest. I don't want any more of those boxes arriving long after his death, full of our letters and photos, his odds and ends.

JIMMY DID NOT win my red marble. I was, after all, the marble champion of the world. I won his green swirly marble, and several yellow ones. After our game, we sat on the curb. The afternoon had grown colder.

"You got my favorite," Jimmy said.

"Which one is that?"

"The green one."

I looked at him, then at the marble, which was a glorious green.

"I want that marble." Jimmy's voice was not soft and hushed. His voice was hard sounding, and cold.

In the middle of the game for Jimmy's green marble, just before his shot, Jimmy said, "My Dad is in the Army."

I looked up. "My Dad flies."

"They knew each other," Jimmy said, shooting. His shot went wide. "My Dad is in Africa. Where's yours?"

"I don't know," I said. I thought he was in England, but we hadn't heard from him in a while. I rolled my shooter between my palms, the warmth of it, its smoothness, soothing me.

"How come you don't know?" Jimmy asked. He was picking at a weed in the pavement, and he looked bony, with one round knee stuck up under his chin and his thin fingers reaching for that weed.

"I heard something. You want to hear it?" I asked.

Jimmy nodded. He pulled up the weed.

"I heard that in Maine there are German bodies washing up on shore. It's true," I said. "Men shot down over the sea."

Jimmy looked at me then, weed in hand, and I stared back, suddenly uncomfortable. The neighborhood seemed silent, or maybe that's memory faltering. I do remember that I stopped the game and handed Jimmy his green marble. I don't know what made me decide to hand the marble back. Maybe the idea of having a friend appealed, or of doing a good deed. Maybe the idea of falling planes made me superstitious as well as charitable. *If I give the marble back, then...*

"What's your dad do in those planes?" Jimmy asked.

"He navigates," I said.

THE WAR I remember is the war for the bathroom, for breakfast, for company. I waited for the bathroom in the mornings while the older girls styled their hair and brushed on rouge. I squeezed into my seat at the breakfast table, but I was never done as fast as the others, who were out the door, down the street, before I'd managed to get on my coat.

At 16, Larry was one of the oldest boys I knew. He stashed packs of Camels and Lucky Strikes in the springs under his bed and in the baseball trophy cups on his book shelf. I watched him hide the packs, standing look out by the door, and admired his ingenuity. He never asked me not to tell. He called me "sport".

On summer nights he slipped out his second story window to the soft earth below and crept across the lawn. I never slept until I knew he'd hit the ground safely, made his escape. I heard a soft thud, a laugh and a low whistle, and I'd think, he's gone now.

In the morning, he'd be the first one up. He'd wink at me, and I'd smile and shake my head and wonder how he got back up the bare white shingles. I'd watch him comb his hair with the part on the side, and I'd try to keep up with him when he took the stairs two by two, but I never could.

Thank God for Jimmy, who waited for me at his house, two houses down, diagonal from ours. He'd watch out the window, and when he saw me emerge, he'd open his front door and meet me on the sidewalk. We traded lunches as we walked to school. We talked about the war. *If I was there, this war would be over. If I were there, we'd be in Berlin right now. If.* We sat in school and drew pictures in our notebooks and waited to be old.

JIMMY'S MOTHER GOT a job, so my mother agreed to feed Jimmy dinner, look in on him when he was sick, walk him home at nine when his mother finally pulled in their drive.

Usually, I'd come home from school with Jimmy in tow. Tommy Ocerly would come over later with John Swenson, and all of us would be together for the afternoons, afternoons that seemed to stretch forever. We played Hide Behind Enemy Lines and Be a Spy and Capture a German flag. Later, Tommy and John would fade into the dusk, and we would sit, Jimmy and I, and wait to be called inside, not wanting to go, wanting to sit in the coming dark.

Larry came home after practice, when the sky was getting dark. He played football and baseball, and Jimmy and I would watch him stroll up the sidewalk, books under one arm, his walk long and easy. We'd wait until Larry got about a block away and then call out to him.

"How was practice?"

"Practice was fine. How was school?"

And school was never exciting. We hadn't learned anything, we would tell him, and we were tired of going. Our
conversation never varied. We'd wait for him to reach us, and
then we would walk inside together, to a kitchen crowded
with women and light.

After dinner we'd gather in the living room. We would hear
Edward R. Murrow introduce himself from London, hear the
funny sounding names of battle grounds and try to remember
the pronunciation. We'd hear the names of generals, men like
Montgomery and DeGaulle, hear the names so often that we
took possession of them, spoke as if we knew them. We would
say things like, That Montgomery is a good man. Or, good
luck to you, DeGaulle. Or, get him, MacArthur.

I knew these men better than my father.

THE DAY JIMMY did not meet me to walk to school, I walked
alone. His mother's car was in the driveway. I knocked on the
front door, but no one answered. Nothing stirred. That afternoon I told my mother that Jimmy had missed school and that
his mother's car was in the drive, and she bit her lip. I went
outside, out of habit. Tommy floated across his yard, John
trailing behind him, and we waited for Jimmy.

"Wonder where he is," John said.

"Isn't he sick today?" Tommy asked.

We knew his wasn't an absence due to sickness. My mother

looked in on him when he was sick. There was a new silence in our world then.

"Want to play Capture the Flag?" John asked.

I shook my head no, and Tommy agreed.

Then Tommy said, "I guess we better go."

I sat by myself, watching Jimmy's house. I was silent later as Larry turned up our road, walked toward me. He stopped when he saw me.

"Where's Jimmy?" he asked.

I shrugged and licked my lips.

Larry looked over at Jimmy's house. Then he said, "Come on, Dolores."

But I wouldn't move.

"Come on, Dolores."

I shook my head.

And so Larry sat with me. We sat as the sky deepened into a dark blue, then black; sat as the shades slipped down windows along the street. We watched the stars come out. My mother opened the door and called to us, but neither of us answered, and I heard the door close, and still we sat.

Finally Larry said, "We'll go talk to him tomorrow. Let's go inside, okay, sport? We'll make sure he's okay tomorrow."

Larry took me by the hand. He walked me inside the house. He said, "You're a good friend, Dolores."

The next day Jimmy reappeared, ashen and smaller looking, and said his Dad wasn't coming home. He met us on the way to school, me and Tommy and John, all of us walking together for a change. Jimmy had his hands in his pockets, and we all stood on the curb. I looked at the sky, and I think Tommy and John looked at the ground, and Jimmy was so quiet that for a moment I forgot he was there, forgot why I was watching the clouds. The beginning of a thought nagged at me, and I shook my head, shook away the thought.

"Did he get shot?" John asked.

Jimmy spoke clearly. "He got shot a bunch of times."

LARRY LEFT ON a cold winter day in January. A heavy snow had fallen throughout the night, but he was up and out the door despite the weather. He did not say good-bye. He did not write a note. I woke to a quiet morning and trudged downstairs, heavy with sleep. I ate my oatmeal and listened to Grammy call him.

"He's probably in the bathroom," I mumbled.

But Linda was the one in the bathroom.

Grammy called again and again, and I remember her voice like an echo through the house, not fading as she climbed the stairs but growing louder with each call, with each thick silence that followed.

I put my spoon down and listened to her call his name. I looked out the window at the soft snow, and I thought, he's gone. He would soon be with them, in those funny sounding places, and I envied him.

From then on, it was just Jimmy and me. We still sat on the curb, and we still lingered in the cool night air after we were called inside. We still played with Tommy and John, but the games were suddenly urgent. We tackled each other to defend our flag. We shot whoever played the Germans again and again and again, standing over each other, sometimes placing a foot down on a shoulder, pressing. We died for our country a hundred times.

JIMMY'S DAD'S DOG tags came on a day when the snow had fallen and my boots were wet on the inside and the sky was gray like ash. I asked Jimmy what they were.

"This is what my Dad wore to identify himself. This is how they knew it was him lying there."

I wanted to ask more questions, but Jimmy started crying, and so I sat beside him and was quiet. The afternoon was cold, and in between his sobs, Jimmy shivered, his body trembling.

My father seemed vague and shadowy to me already. I didn't think I could lose him any more than I had, but I saw those tags, and touched them, and they were hard and smooth and warm from Jimmy's constant agitation of them, and I knew this: that I could lose my father completely, and so when my mother came to me one day, and pulled me down to her side, and told me in a choked voice that his plane had not come back, I was not surprised. He was shot down over the North Sea, she said. I didn't know where that was, but that didn't matter. I imagined, as she kept talking, that my father was deep inside the sea, in his plane, and that he was silent there. I sat and held her hand. I didn't cry, but I know that at that moment my father's absence became a part of me, a defining feature, like an extra finger or toe.

My father's dog tags never came. After what seemed like a long time, I asked my mother why. She was washing dishes after dinner. Grammy was at the table with her sewing kit, patching pants, and Linda was doing her math, and Jimmy was staring at the tablecloth, and I asked.

"When am I going to get Dad's dog tags?"

Jimmy looked up, suddenly interested. My mother stared out the window above the kitchen sink. She had bags under her eyes.

"Dolly," she said, "you won't ever get his dog tags."

Nothing else was said, but as everyone filtered into the living room, Jimmy and I sat at the table, each of us staring into our laps. We said nothing. Jimmy did not express sympathy, nor did I ask for it, but he didn't rub his tags as we sat at the kitchen table. We were just together there, listening to the murmur of Edward R. Murrow.

A new image came to me. I saw a cascading fireball, doused

by salt water. I saw my father, all of him, whoever he was, those tags, descending hot and red and splintered into the cool relief of the sea.

IN THE END, most of the men did come home, Joey and Ray and Larry and the others my mother doesn't name. When Uncle Ray stepped out of the car, I didn't know who he was. Later I looked at the photographs and decided he didn't look a thing like himself. I noticed the red on his cheeks, the way his hair looked lighter, and I knew somebody had touched up the photograph.

Jimmy and I stood apart from everybody and watched Linda reach for Uncle Ray's hand, and glad as we were to see Ray, we would have traded him in a minute. We waved the little American flags Grammy handed us. We cheered when Ray climbed out of the car and stood, blinking, at the welcome home sign we had hung from the second story windows. Then Jimmy drifted slowly backwards, still waving his flag, and I drifted with him. Nobody noticed. We walked into the backyard and over the fence and on and on. I started to run, and I ran as fast and as far as I could, with Jimmy at my heels.

Grammy's household split back up into smaller ones. My mother and I stayed with Grammy. We were the ones who were still incomplete, missing a part that should have been there, and so we kept together.

16

It wasn't long after Grammy's house split up that Jimmy's mother decided to move back home to Missouri. I watched Jimmy and his mother drive away. I was eight years old. I sat down on the curb and waved as the back end of their DeSoto turned the corner. Jimmy did not wave back. Maybe he was rubbing those tags. Maybe he was crying. I didn't cry, not then. The front door opened and Uncle Ray, whose voice was low and rumbly like an engine, called to me.

He said, "Dolores."

His voice rose at the end, like I was a question.

I WONDER NOW if Jimmy's tags still exist, or if he has rubbed them completely away. I am sitting on the curb at dusk, as we used to do, and I'm holding a letter in my hand. A childhood friend, a girl from school, is visiting England, and she sent me a note. I usually hear from her at Christmas, a card, or sometimes a phone call if she's back in Kansas. On her trip, she visited Cambridge, where there is a memorial chapel for all those who died in the war and were never found. In scanning the list of names in the stone, she found my father's. Anthony Jason Jones. She sent me a rubbing.

GROWING UP COLD

IN THE COLD night air, my breath is like mist. I stand at the end of the driveway with my hands in my jeans pockets and my head tilted back, watching each breath cloud, then disappear. Above me, the moon is pale and the stars are faint, as if even they are shrinking from the chill.

This far north of the Twin Cities street lights are few, and in the darkness landmarks meld with the landscape. The shape of the Marshall's nineteenth century farmhouse is vague, as is the jagged, low expanse of their wood fence, though both are just across the road. A row of young elm trees runs behind the fence in a neat and even line, save one, which leans into its neighbor as if it's relieved to share the burden of once having stood upright. Occasionally a breeze rises and knocks branches together. The branches sound like they're cracking and make me feel as if out here, in the calm of night, I am actually hearing the cold.

My older sister Lonnie died here a few days ago, crumpled inside an old VW van. My father and brother heard the crash, a sound they have not described but which I can imagine, like a pop can being neatly compacted, like the sound of my father's voice on the phone, compressing into silence and the faint whisper of my reply, that yes of course I would come home. And so I came back to this brittle, quiet place and our brittle, quiet house.

There aren't many travelers tonight. No one on the way to church or 4H or the new movie theater out in Stern. No one coming here, though I suppose they will arrive tomorrow, a steady stream of sedans and Hondas and beaten up trucks because Lonnie had a light inside her, an exuberance, that even our fucked up family couldn't quite kill.

The road stretches into the darkness. Across the way, the lights are out in the Marshall's' house. They have gone to Florida, in search of warmth. And it is desolate here, in the dark with the occasional wind and the snow and the endless cold. It is a different version of hell.

At my feet, I have a large collection of sparklers and candles and a dented Nike shoebox with Lonnie's picture inside. The plastic noisemakers I brought home from Japan are spilling out of a bag, looking festive on the hard packed snow and ice, promising some kind of party. I have my bottle of choice tucked safely inside my coat. If Lonnie were here, there would be some kind of party, but now they serve a new purpose, one that has driven me out of the house, to the edge of the road. Here.

Tonight I pulled in at dusk, the tires hushed against the snow, my headlights giving the terrain a lunar cast. Dad had the house lit up, and I had watched it loom as I drove that last stretch of road, waiting for the distance to disappear. Dad met me at the front door and took my duffel and patted me on the shoulder. We had not seen each other for two years, and he looked small, standing there with his lined face and watery eyes and white beard. He looked bent. He said, "Welcome home, John" and his welcome sounded tired and faint and strange, stranger still without Lonnie bounding down the stairs, long brown hair flying, hand wrapped around the banister as if to brake herself.

I had hoped that James would be waiting, too, but it was a short time before he appeared, circling into the kitchen later and pulling up a chair. He of the immaculate hair and square jaw, the raw looks of a rugged movie star. After two years, he held out a hand.

"You're getting brawny," he said.

I had nothing to say, caught short again.

We collected under the flat, pooled light of the kitchen lamp, elbows on the table, and we settled for the old familiar. *How's the business? How're the Marshall's?* Trust James, though, to throw a spanner into the calm of my return with an abrupt announcement about the funeral. Father Andresen would be conducting the service, he said, his comment running over a casual discussion about the temperature.

I looked at him then. His eyes seemed hard and without a flicker of light. He tapped his fingers on the table, waiting.

I have a particular dislike for Father Andresen, but that isn't his point. His point is that I usually avoid what I dislike. School, people, social obligations. And James knows that my having come all this way does not mean I will be at Lonnie's funeral tomorrow.

And he's right.

I am not sure I could bear it, and I'm not sure Lonnie would mind at all if I were to choose a very different farewell and leave it at that.

I meet James' gaze. *Blink first*, I think. *You relentless fucker.*

Dad is saying something to me, and I nod, but I keep my gaze fixed on James. It has been two years, and only one thing has changed. Lonnie is not here to buffer us.

THE LAST TIME I went to church willingly, I was ten years old. Lonnie was sixteen and James was eighteen, and we were attending our mother's funeral. I sat in the pew and avoided looking at her casket. I counted the variety of flowers in the altar bouquets. Eleven. I stared at my shoes while Father Andresen droned on. It was his drone that got to me, the tired way he mustered his eulogy. And the stain on his sleeve as he had greeted me that morning. And the look in his eyes, as if he was trying to remember my mother amidst all his quiet volunteers and committed housewives. The little one with the mop of hair and the loud laugh, I wanted to tell him. A laugh like a waterfall. She was the lady who made banana bread for your church fairs.

At the house later, as family and friends milled about the living room whispering condolences, my father came to find me. I was sitting on the hood of somebody's station wagon, looking out into the woods behind the house. Dad joined me. He asked if I was okay, and I told him no. He patted me on the back then and tried to form a sentence, maybe only a word, but no sound came out.

From then on, we had arguments every Sunday morning about whether or not I was going to church, arguments which he felt justified our attendance. From then on, each Sunday until I grew too big, he grabbed me by the neck or shoulders or arm and dragged me to the car. In church we sat side by side, with Lonnie on my other side and James on his. We sat in silent row, separated by a breath and yet a whole world.

My mother choked to death on a peanut butter sandwich.

The day was a Saturday. We were eating a pick-up lunch together, and then we were watching my father push against her stomach, watching her slump in his arms, watching him pound on her back when even we knew pounding didn't matter.

I PULL A bottle of Jack Daniels from underneath my down jacket and take a long drink. Then another. No, I don't think I will go to the funeral tomorrow. I'm going to honor my sister my way.

I imagine James lurking in the house, watching the clock and wondering what I'm doing out here. I don't know why he cares. And I imagine that what I'm about to do might annoy him and my Dad, but it would only be the latest in a long string of disappointments and failures. Skipping church. Failing English. Drinking too much. Totaling my car on Highway 80. Pretending to apply to colleges. Leaving for Japan. Leaving suddenly, like it was an escape. And for me it was.

So what further damage could one small, bright, tiny explosion of color do?

I line my candles up in the snow and light them. The candles are different colors, blue and red and a waxy yellow. I intersperse the sparklers, then stand and take another drink. I spin one of my noisemakers around, and the noise carries in the cold, grating and harsh. Tonight I'm going to give Lonnie the best damn farewell I can, just me and my firecrackers, the stars and the snow. Tonight I'm going to stage my own Obon.

Nori-chan told me about August 15th, The Night of the Last Day of Obon. He was a student in my English class for Nagasaki businessmen. He said that families who have lost a member during the preceding year carry a float through the streets of Nagasaki to honor their dead. Until their families put their relatives on the path to heaven, the souls of the dead wander in limbo. After Obon, the souls may return home for the first time. They are free.

On August 15th, in the cool of dusk, we gathered. I stood next to Nori-chan on the curb outside the Prefectural Office, at the crest of the hill, which was near the end of the parade route. From the Prefectural Office the road was a straight shot down the hill into Nagasaki Harbor. The hill was crowded, and I jostled for position, bumping Nori and knocking ash off the tip of his cigarette, holding my Kirin high above my head so the beer wouldn't spill. Firecrackers exploded in pops at our feet, and in the distance trails of smoke marked pathways in the sky. Nori smoked his cigarettes one after the other as the day gave way. He said, in Japanese, "As soon as it's dark."

Lonnie lent me most of the money for my plane ticket to Tokyo. She said, "If you need to do this, then go." I was 18 and lucky. I landed a job teaching in a dusty, cramped, second-rate language school and was gone for two straight years.

I came back to the States a month ago and settled up in Thunder Bay because I love the name. I came back and unpacked and before I could visit, Lonnie drove into a tree. At seventy miles an hour. Straight down the hill by our house on an icy road and suddenly, no brakes. She was rushing home because she was late for James' birthday dinner.

EARLIER THIS EVENING, Dad came and sat on the end of my bed as I unpacked. He watched me hang up my dark wool suit, my white shirt.

"Where'd you get those?"

"Hong Kong."

"When did you go to Hong Kong?"

"During a school break in Japan," I said. "I went for a week."

"I didn't know you went to Hong Kong."

I shrugged. "I didn't think you'd be interested."

"Of course I'm interested." His voice sounded gruff. "I've always been interested."

I hung the clothes on the rack and turned, uncertain what to say.

We were silent for what seemed like a long time, and then he said, "Will you stay for a few days?"

I paused, unpacked my comb, and ran my fingers up and down its teeth. "Yes."

"James is having nightmares."

"I'm sorry about that." And I am sorry for him. I know a lot about those.

Dad turned at the door, looked above my head to I don't know where. "Do you want to say anything for Lonnie at the funeral?"

There was a pause, a moment without sound, and then I shook my head no, wondering if I'd be there or if I'd already be back on the road, heading anywhere.

"You're coming to the funeral, aren't you?" he asked. He was still looking away and above me, and for a second, in a quick breath, I wanted to say yes even if it might not be true, but I said nothing.

He looked right at me then, his eyes watery and tinged with yellow. He said, softly, "Please."

I DRIFTED AWAY from the house as soon as I could tonight. Dad stared at my shoebox and bag but asked nothing. All he said was, "It's cold out there." I don't mind cold. I've always felt safest when my ass is half frozen. I always feel, despite the cold, like I'm warm.

Inside the house Dad and James huddle together in the living room: James sitting in the rocking chair with his bottle of Glenfiddich on one knee and a glass of water on the other; Dad looking out the living room window across the backyard to the woods. They're waiting, like I am, but I can't stand company when I wait for things. I usually can't stand company at all.

Out here, by the road, the snow drifts are thigh high on me, which means they must rival the elementary school kids in height. I think of this now, of kids dressed in their jackets and mittens and scarves, waiting for the school bus to lumber and shake its way down the hill. I think of them standing in sub-zero temperatures every morning, wrapped in wool and Thinsulate. Growing up cold.

I grew up cold. We all did. We grew up shivering.

In a few hours, the light will sweep away the darkness. Slowly, the kids will congregate. They'll shiver here, near where I stand now, until the bus gets down the hill. While they wait, they'll probably look at our house, at the drawn curtains and the abundance of cars in the driveway, and whisper about Miss Lindstrom. One of the older kids will point out the thin, leaning tree, and a few kids will look at the break, then eye the hill, still glossy with ice. And I'll be in my room, convincing myself to stay.

In Thunder Bay I live alone in an old house, where I am house-sitting. Pretty soon I'll have to go. I've heard through a carpenter friend of mine that there's opportunity to work with him in Anchorage, that I might be able to save up, eventually buy land, and build myself a house. Get away from civilization, which sounds pretty damn good. Leaving now, for anywhere, sounds pretty damn good. I use my bottle of Jack to balance and kick at a bare spot in the ground. The earth is hard and unyielding, and I wonder if staying matters, if we'll be able to bury Lonnie after all.

LONNIE USED TO drive a 1972 green VW bus named Fred. The back end was covered with Dead decals and Democratic candidate bumper stickers and rust. Freddie was in constant need of repair, but Lonnie wouldn't give up on him. She called Dad or James whenever Freddie broke down. Last week, she had called James to fix the brakes, and he went right over.

Lonnie never drove Fred to school. Didn't suit a teacher, she said. Instead, she drove Mom's aging Oldsmobile, which Dad had never had the heart to sell. For me, the car brought back memories. My mother, scarf wrapped carefully around her head to protect her new, smelly, perfect curls. Memories of Mom and me rushing home from school, from anywhere, barreling down the road with the windows down, and singing. Singing anything, sometimes yelling, for the sheer joy of making noise.

Lonnie said that the Oldsmobile never brought back memories for her. She also said she liked the comfortable habit of church. But whenever I was around, she slept in on Sundays, and we planned day trips to Stillwater and Lake Superior. She climbed up on the roof with me if the weather was warm and got stoned. She drove Fred.

I want Lonnie back, and my mother, who had a gift for

laughter. But before Lonnie, before even my mother, I first loved James, and I would like him back, too.

TONIGHT DAD MADE a list of people to ask back to the house. He gave the list to James to call.

"Who are these people?" I had asked, looking over James' shoulder. I didn't recognize more than a few.

"Friends of ours from church," he said.

"Are any of Lonnie's friends coming?" I asked.

James scowled at me. "Of course," he said.

I wanted to ask who on the list was a friend, but his look stopped me. James always stops me.

When we were young, James and I used to ride along the road past Marshall's farm, down to the footpath, and back into the woods to Meyer's Creek, where we'd swim. We used to camp in the yard, me and James. He taught me how to ride. He taught me my knots for Cub Scouts.

But then we lost Mom, we sold the horses to Marshall, and James went down to the U of M and fell in love. When he came home on breaks, he didn't want to swim in Meyer's Creek. He wasn't interested in camping in the yard. Once I asked him to walk with me to the creek to see a small waterfall I'd found. He said no thanks. He wanted to talk to Dad about courses and grades and security. He talked about taking over the business. Feed supply.

Her name was Cathy, and she came home with James a few times, but then she stopped visiting. James moved home. He started working with Dad. He got quiet. He hassled me about my longish hair, my grades, my tendency to mess around. My drinking, which began early. Everything. Lonnie mediated or kept us apart. She'd run around with me, take spur of the moment drives to Minneapolis, but she always kept us within boundaries, like the state lines. She'd never drive all the way to Mexico, which was what I wanted. Then she went to the U. She hardly ever came to visit, and when she finally moved back home, I couldn't believe she actually had.

I offered to help with the calls to church friends, but James waved me away.

"I know these people," he said.

"Is there anything I can do?" I asked.

"Be there," he said, without looking up. He dialed another number, then glanced up at me as he waited through the ring. I held his gaze, a flood of memories coming back. His neatly pressed shirts. His careful, small scribbles in Dad's ledger. A cramped and careful life that allowed no surprises or idle moments. Not even me, so long ago. Nothing at all.

AT DARK THE floats appeared, as Nori had promised. Huge floats, carried on poles that crossed underneath the bottom, carried by men and women dressed in happi coats and white shorts. Relatives, Nori said, and family friends, one of whom walked in front of the float, guiding the float to heaven. They handed out candy as they passed. They threw firecrackers onto the street.

The floats were the size of boats but wider, shaped like teardrops on each end, with pictures of the deceased hung high in the back. The photographs were black and white, the faces somber and without smiles; and as the floats passed, the faces loomed above us. The floats were trimmed with flowers; lighted paper lanterns hung inside. On the front of each, painted in black kanji on white paper, were the names of the dead.

There was a Big Bird float for a dead child, no picture; then a pair of boats for a young couple; an elderly man who walked along the edge of the crowd on the opposite side of the street. He carried a small float in his arms, walked with his head bent over it, as if to protect the float from the smoke and ash. He carried his farewell in his arms.

Firecrackers exploded constantly in the street, in the air, and we laughed as the ash peppered our hair. The smoke became thick, and still the floats came, still the march for the dead continued, late into the night. When the last float passed us, our ears were ringing. Smoke filled the air like fog. We brushed ash from our hair, our shoulders. We walked home as ash fell. We walked home in a city as silent as dawn. And as we walked, the families carried the floats down the hill to water's edge and threw them into the harbor.

On August 16th, no one in Nagasaki is allowed to swim.

AFTER DAD'S BRIEF visit to my room earlier tonight, James knocked on my door and walked on in. "Can I talk to you?"

"Sure." I was sitting on my bed, rifling through my duffel for the Nike shoebox. "What's up?"

"I came to ask you to come to the funeral tomorrow."

He is tall, James. Tall and lean. His shirt hung off his shoulders, and the baggy style thinned him.

"I'll try."

"It would be nice if we could count on you, John." He sounded bitter.

"James, I'll try."

"What's your problem? She's your sister, and she's dead, and we're burying her tomorrow. I don't get it. How do you think she'd feel if she knew you blew off her funeral?"

"I think she'd understand."

"Well, I don't."

"The point is, James, that she would."

We stared at each other, and then he shook his head.

"John, if you're not there, I swear . . . -"

I cut him off. "Get out." I heard a voice I had not heard in years, the one I reserved just for him. Civil, crisp. He seemed about to speak again so I did instead. "Go. Now."

My candles are burning brightly now, and I look to the road, up toward where the hill should be. Suddenly I want to be at the crest of that hill, where she was in that breath before the bus started down, gathering speed. I want to imagine what she saw of this house.

The road is still sheathed in ice. The cold reaches to my bones, but I don't care. I climb slowly, slowly, reach for a rock, anything solid, and pull myself to the top. From the crest of the hill, I stare down at the blinking lights that are my candles. I see only candlelight and house lights, stars and the dull, muted yellow of a winter moon. I think of Lonnie, tuck my bottle inside my coat, and as the breeze rises again and whips cold air and snow around me, I scream. My scream fills the night, carries to my Obon, to wherever Lonnie is, and then I rush forward, moving as fast as I can, and charge down the hill. I slip on the ice and roll to the bottom over gravel and ice and hard-packed snow. At the bottom, I curl and listen to the stillness, and I wonder what she thought as the brake gave way, as everything blurred.

I'm walking back to my candles when I hear the crisp thwack of the front door closing, then my name spoken tentatively into the chill night air.

"James." My voice is a whisper. I stand by my Obon, brush off the snow. Suddenly he is at my side, no coat on, and I hear my father's heavy, crunching footsteps fast approaching.

"Are you okay?" James asks.

"Yeah."

"You just felt like screaming?"

"What happened?" Dad asks, but his question gets lost because James is looking at my Obon, and I'm suddenly too tense to answer.

"What is this?"

I turn away. I wish I hadn't screamed. That I wasn't back here. That I had never tried. I take a sip of Jack.

"Will you leave that bottle alone? You're...-"

I eyeball him. "Stop."

Dad steps between us, holding up his hands. James takes a step back, but as he does so, he says, "You're one hell of a drunk, John."

I turn back around. "And you, James, are one hell of a mechanic."

He comes at me too fast. I'm slammed down hard on the driveway and out of breath before I can think. He hits me hard. He pins me down and reaches for my bottle. He pulls at the bottle, pulls until finally I don't give a damn and I let the bottle go and pound him in the ribs.

I hit him for every time he told me my hair was too long,

for every time he complained about my skipping church or my messy room or that my late nights were way too late. But I hit him hardest for not going to Meyer's Creek to see the waterfall. I was little then, and lonely. I had needed him, and he had said no thanks. In the background I hear my father yelling for us to stop, but stopping isn't on my list of priorities right now. I just want to pound James. I want to hit his complaints out of him one by one. I want all the things that James says I am not to be silenced by who I am, and so I hit him harder. I hit until my arms lose their strength and fall heavily, one at my side, the other across his back. I am still no match for him. My arm is around him, sort of, and he's still swinging, and I let him swing into my ribs, my face, and then I just hold on.

My father is tugging on James and finally pulls him off me. "Stop it," Dad says. " Stop."

James is sobbing. Dad pulls him to his feet, says, "Go inside. For God's sake, James."

I hear James' boots scrape across the snow. His steps are uneven, heavy, slow.

Dad stands above me, and I see he's wearing his thick old, shit kicker boots. He squats down to my level. He stares at my row of candles and sparklers, at my noisemakers, at my bottle of Jack. I sit up. My face is a mess; my ribs ache.

"Your lip is bleeding," Dad says, and his voice is like a sigh. He tries to wipe the blood off my lip. "We've got to stick together."

He isn't talking to me, but I answer him anyway. "Well, we've never been very good at that."

"We've tried, John," he says. "In our own ways, we've tried."

My head aches. My sides ache. I see my bottle and pick it up. Broken. Suddenly I don't care. I wonder what the hell I'm becoming.

"Come inside," Dad says, and he pulls me up by the arms. He starts to lead me up the driveway.

I don't want to go inside. I want to build a float for Lonnie. A loud, noisy, smoking float shaped like a teardrop. No, I want the float to be shaped like a green VW bus. I want to say good-bye my way, in one loud fucking sayonara. I want to watch her soul bob along with everybody else's, just bounce and drift along to heaven, or wherever, to the sea. I want to get drunk and say good-bye with fireworks. I want ash to fall in my hair, as though her body, all the bodies, have suddenly rocketed like firecrackers into the sky above me, above the noise, and then down through the smoke and the alcohol onto all of us who're still stuck here.

Maybe I've been speaking out loud because Dad lets go of my arm. He says, "Hold on."

I can't move without pain. I'm staring at my candles, at the flames. The colors are melting into the snow. The breeze comes again, a whisper of ice against my face. I take Lonnie's picture out of the shoebox and set it on top. Then I bend down to light the candles that are snuffed out. Dad puts his hands on his knees and bends down beside me. I ignore him. I strike a match against the matchbox, but the match breaks. I reach for a second.

"What're you doing, John?"

"A Japanese thing I saw once." I try to explain, but I realize I can't quite move my hand, that I can't quite move my lips.

I try a third match. I'm running out. Dad picks up a noisemaker, twists it around, and the sound is as cold as the temperature.

"I want you to know something," he says. "I want you to know that I gave Lonnie most of the money that got you to Japan."

I stop, hand in mid-air, the match lit. Our eyes meet. He looks away.

"I told her not to tell you. She wanted to, but I said no. I don't know why." Dad shrugs.

The match burns down. Takes me a minute to feel the sting. I drop the match in the snow, and then I can't do anything. My head is spinning, and my hands. My fingers. Numb.

I scan the sky, looking across the whole shitty expanse of black for a light or a star or a constellation which will tell me where to go from here. But I've never been good with constellations; I've never been good at finding my way, and I know now, sitting here in the dead cold of winter, that I may never change.

We are side by side. Dad takes the matches from my hand. His hands are red, and he quickly pulls the match along the box. Slowly, methodically, he lights candle after candle. Red, blue, yellow, red, blue. Then he lights the sparklers.

We watch the sparklers fire up, then fizzle in turn. The last sparkler dies out, and then we stare at the candles, at the rainbow snow. The breeze sends cold air against my skin like a whip. The cold burns. I look over at my father, who's staring into the flames.

"Arigato goziamashta." My voice sounds thick.

He looks at me, lips parted. He doesn't understand my thank you in Japanese, but he's nodding when he turns to look at my Obon.

"All right then," he says. He is aging, curving under the weight of grief and years, and he asks, "What do we do next?"

Then he picks up a noisemaker and hands me the other. He twists his noisemaker once, the sound like tearing cloth, and I join in, and then we twist the noisemakers round and round and round, 'til the sound is all I can hear, and the sound is my goodbye.

POINTS OF EXCHANGE

I LASTED ONLY SIX months in New York, an amount of
time that embarrassed me at first. Humiliated me, actually.
I never planned to come back to Minnesota, to live again in
this gaggle of women, in a world off-balance, uneven, full of
unasked for advice and long conversations over coffee, full of
permanents and hair coloring, high heels and perfume, ortho-
pedic shoes and hot flashes. And sweat. Calluses on the hands
and broken down cars that no one knows how to fix. I worked
hard not to move home after college graduation. I wanted to
escape, get out, go far away to a place where there was more
than women, an abundance of lakes and long O's dragged out
in nasal. I ended up on Avenue C.

In New York, I lived by a stop sign, and in my neighborhood, that meant I lived at the point of exchange. I lived above

the street, on the third floor, but sounds came to me clearly: the whine of the M15 bus as it slowed to a stop; the occasional burst of rap from a passing car; and Rashon, always Rashon.

I'd hear Rashon outside early in the mornings, and she'd still be there when the streetlights came on, singing her songs and finishing her hundredth game of hopscotch for the day. She looked small to me, little, as though she might be only ten years old, and day after day she played hopscotch in the same blue windbreaker, pale blue like the sky, wearing the same brown sandals and what looked like the same plaid jumper and navy knee-high socks.

Each morning when I left for work, I'd say hello to her, and she never replied. Once, though, she stopped mid-game and stared at me as I tore out of my building. I was late. I said good morning, and she didn't answer, and after I passed her, she yelled, "Who're you?" I turned. She stood with her hands on her hips, and it was odd, suddenly, not to see her moving, to see her standing still.

"My name is Jenny," I said. "What's yours?"

Rashon threw her hands in the air then and tossed her stone back over her head. She didn't check to see where the stone landed. Her arms fell. She didn't move again, and she didn't answer. She stared me into movement of my own. I took a small step back, turned and walked to the bus stop, fast.

I worked in a trade publishing company, where the manuscripts that passed under my nose did so primarily because I was photocopying them. I hadn't expected the job to be more than it was, but I wanted life to be. After four years at a small college in the middle of Vermont, I wanted what my freshman college roommate, Corrie, called the world in one neighborhood.

"Where I grew up," she had said, "half the neighborhood speaks Spanish, a third speak English, and the rest speak Polish."

By graduation, Corrie had yet to find a job. She did, however, have her parents' co-op apartment. They had moved outside the city. She said, "Come live with me. It's the cheapest housing you'll find." So I did.

We lived in Alphabet City, a name I thought was quaint until I drove into the neighborhood on a steaming day in June. Litter lined the gutters, and a homeless man lay sprawled across the pavement in front of a liquor store. On the light post nearby, fluttering in the breeze, was a brightly colored sign that read: We're proud of Avenue C.

I didn't go out much, given my salary, and I spent too many nights at home, reading manuscripts. When my eyes got tired, I slipped underneath the blinds in my bedroom, pressed my head against the cool glass, and stared down at the street. On the hottest nights, I'd open the window and let the sounds of the place roll into my room, take over. I'd smell whatever 2F cooked for dinner. Baked chicken. Polenta with spicy red sauce. Fettuccine Alfredo. 2F lived off Fettuccine Alfredo.

The cars that came down the avenue came slowly. I'd hear a car before I saw it, catch the low booming sound of overdone bass, see light fan out on the blacktop, and then slowly, around the corner, a car. At the stop sign, if the car paused, a shape would emerge from the shadows, step forward, lean in. I stepped back from the window then.

The co-op buildings rose high into the air on either side of a pedestrian mall. Our building was on the corner, as was our apartment, and although my bedroom faced the street, our living room faced the mall. The mall was concrete, but grass grew on each side and daisies bloomed as a border. Three wooden benches lined the mall on one side, spaced out evenly along the concrete, and at the far end, toward Avenue D, was a school. The school had an overhang that stretched out into the school yard, a square, cement plaza with three benches and a garbage can stuck into the concrete.

At night, teenage boys hung out in packs in the school yard. On the nights I came home late from work, I saw the boys standing in clumps under the overhang, away from the street lights. Yet there were nights I'd turn into the mall, and the boys were on the move, an army dressed in dark jeans and dark sweatshirts and on cold days, heavy quilted jackets, the hoods lined with fake fur. Cigarettes, high tops, gold chains. Sometimes African-American, sometimes white, sometimes Chicano, sometimes all three. They walked quietly, right down the mall, and I never understood what caused them to spring into action. I never caught the sign.

My MOTHER KNEW I wouldn't like New York. Then again, she always knew everything. New York was the last city out of fifteen I had listed in a survey from my college career office. The survey asked, where would you like to live? I put Boston first, then London and Paris. I had, in fact, written down Peoria over New York and been serious.

But I hated that my mother knew.

Mom and her boyfriend, Earl, had called me on my first night in New York. Mom wanted to know if I was okay. Earl wanted to wish me good luck. He wanted me to know how exciting New York was, how wonderful. "Go to the Blue Note," he said, "and the Metropolitan Opera. Do you like opera?"

Earl loved opera. He especially loved "The Pearl Fishers." Stout, quiet Earl, who worked in a Volvo repair shop and sang the Gopher fight song while watching TV basketball games; Earl, who hunted ducks with Uncle Ray. He said he liked to sing arias in the shower, and then he laughed, and then his voice trailed off.

I took a breath after I hung up the phone. He'd been trying so hard, so hard that I felt my heart loosen, warm to him. We had both been uncertain, gesturing wildly to the other, waving a white flag as we marched forward to say hello, trying desperately to share the same woman without stepping on each other's toes.

I THINK WHAT drew me to Rashon was that neither of us knew our fathers. That, and the neighborhood. In my home town, everyone knew that my mother came home from California at age eighteen with a belly and no man in tow. I had to go to Girl Scout father-daughter square dances with Uncle Ray, who once busted out of his suit doing the do-si-do. Uncle Ray, who would go out of his way to make the evening special by buying me a corsage. Uncle Ray, whose hand I used to hold, looking away from him, to pretend. But I didn't have to grow up outside, playing hopscotch.

In my hometown, everybody knew my business, and around the co-op apartments, everybody knew Rashon's, or so I learned. Corrie had found a job as a paralegal, and like me, caught the M15 home from work every night. We'd chat on the bus, chat as we walked to the co-op, and one night the subject came around to Rashon.

Neither of us moved fast that evening. On the bus ride home, the air conditioning didn't work, and we nearly stuck to each other in the heat. Work had been long and tedious. My neck ached from hours of proofreading lousy back ad. I wanted air and quiet and for no one to touch me. I wanted to kick the asshole who kept casually rubbing against my butt.

The bus was too crowded for me to turn, but when I climbed off, I looked back. A teenage boy dressed in black jeans and a black T-shirt met my gaze. I gave him a dirty look, but he stared right at me, and then he smirked.

Corrie is a tall, bony woman, with long, straight blonde hair. She carries her height well. She walks with her chin up. She has a command I admire, a quiet way of surveying a scene that gives notice she's arrived, and that night she seemed to glide down the mall, ease her way along, as if nothing could get her down, and I envied her as I struggled to match her pace.

And then there was that same little girl, hair in pigtails, hopping down the hopscotch squares, singing softly to herself, her sandals slapslapslapping against the pavement. She sang slightly off key, on the high side, and I wasn't in the mood for any kind of noise. I wanted her to hit every note or not sing at all.

"Who is that?" I asked.

"That's Rashon."

"I wish she'd shut up for once."

Corrie laughed. "She won't." And then, "You better hope she doesn't 'cause those songs are all she's got."

"What do you mean?"

We paused at the entrance to our building, Corrie casting a slow, frowning glance at Rashon. She shook her head. "She hasn't got much to count on."

Corrie fit her key in the lock, but the lock was broken.

With a snort, she pulled the door open and walked inside. I looked back at Rashon. She hopped to the end of the hopscotch squares, oblivious, it seemed, to an oncoming pack of boys. I put my hand on the door handle and opened it slightly and watched as the boys strutted down the mall, laughing. Rashon landed with both feet in the safety zone and bent down to pick up her stone. When she stood, the boys swarmed around her.

"What you find down there, Rashon?"

"Don't bend over, baby. Not in this neighborhood."

They jostled her, bumping her with their shoulders, and a tall, lanky boy grabbed one of her pigtails. She leaned into his pull. He dragged her to the curb, and she didn't make a sound. The boy let go, and the group went on. I gripped the door handle and swallowed hard. Rashon stared at the pavement, and then she turned, a half turn, and watched the boys walk down toward Avenue B.

"Why isn't anyone watching her?" I asked.

"We were." Corrie shook her head again.

"Where's her mother?"

"Probably sitting on our stairs." Corrie pressed the elevator button and held it.

In the stairways, in the dull, muted lighting, syringes accumulated in the corners of the landings and along the sides of the steps. The stairway was a silent place, no footsteps or voices. Our stairway had a name: the stairway to heaven.

"What about her father?"

Corrie held the elevator door open for me. "He hasn't been around for a long time, and it will be another long time before he is."

"Don't you worry about her?" I asked.

Corrie raised her eyebrows. "Worry?" She paused. "No."

"What if somebody messes with her?"

Corrie rolled her eyes. "Jenny," she said, punching the button for three, "I'm more worried about what will happen if somebody tries to mess with *you*."

Once, I tried to tell my mother about Rashon, about how she sang away the days outside. My words got jumbled. I made no sense. I didn't know, suddenly, what I wanted to tell her. I tried to describe how the neighborhood became another place at night, cooler and dimmer and laced by rap and salsa and sirens, the latter being a music all their own; about how underneath the music, there was a silence I didn't like. At night, when Rashon's mother finally called her inside, the songs stopped, and then there was a stillness in the air, an absence of sound the rap and sirens couldn't hide: the absence of voices. Voices were rare, as if, after dusk, all the people in my neighborhood were holding their breaths.

I'VE NEVER SEEN a picture of my father. My mother said she never took any photos, which made me suspicious. I used to think she hid them from me, and once when I was eight or nine, I sneaked into her bedroom and rifled through her dresser drawers. I carefully sorted through a shoe box full of pictures. Somewhere where I could not find him, there was a man with the same gray eyes like mine, the same square chin, and brown hair, slightly red in the sun, the traits that my mother and grandmother didn't have. He was half of me, the part of myself I didn't know, the part of myself I looked for in a crowd.

Mom came home from work, and there I was, spreading her memories out across her bedroom floor, searching for myself. She sat with me then. She pointed to a photo of my Grandpa, who died shortly before I was born, and she began to recite my story, to give me the details she could, to describe the photos she never took.

"There is not a child in the world more loved than you," my mother always told me, but she couldn't keep emptiness from spreading through me, a feeling so airy I've never forgotten the way it lodged inside me and hung on.

IN EARLY AUGUST, I woke, as usual, to the thwack of feet on pavement, to the high-pitched lyrics of Rashon's songs. She made up a new song each morning, a new theme. Thursday was garbage pick-up day, and Rashon sang loudly about blue plastic garbage cans full of potato peels, banana peels, and apple peels.

I lifted my bedroom blinds and glanced down at the street. The sky was gray with a hint of light. Rashon had drawn her hopscotch game on the sidewalk, not on the mall, and therefore nearer to my room. Her hair was braided in pigtails, which swung back and forth as she hopped from square to square. She hopped to the final square, stretched her legs to avoid a small puddle, turned, and worked her way back, still singing, and loudly. "Garbage, garbage everywhere, gar-bage in the kitchen, gar-bage on the stairs."

I let the blinds fall back into place and curled up in my bed, and still the garbage song came to me clearly through the morning air, carrying above traffic and footsteps. I peeked at my clock. 6 a.m.

My bedroom door opened.

"I'm going to kill her," Corrie said. "I have lived in this neighborhood for twenty-two fucking years, and I haven't had a decent night's sleep anytime I've been home in the last fucking five."

My door closed.

Rashon had finished the whole song and was about to repeat the chorus. I climbed out of bed, stuck my head under the blinds, and opened my window.

"Rashon," I said.

She looked up, still singing.

"Rashon."

She shut up.

"You have to be quiet. People are sleeping, and you're waking them up," I said. "You have officially pissed Corrie off. Do you know Corrie?"

Rashon nodded.

"Good," I said. "Watch out. Today she is going to kill you."

Rashon looked at me. She had her stone in one hand, and she was still as a post. Then she began to swing her arm, and I thought, *oh Jesus.* She swung her arm in a wide arc, and then her whole body started to move. She pointed her toes. She pirouetted. She threw her stone into the squares sketched onto the pavement and danced her way to the safety spot. For a moment, I watched her, and then I shut the window and climbed back into bed. I lay there for another two hours, wide awake, with her song going through my head. I even made up a few lyrics of my own. Yet her silence unnerved me, and in the silence I thought of how a ten-year-old girl from this neighborhood might mistake what was meant as a joke, and I wished I hadn't told her to shut up.

IN SEPTEMBER, RASHON started school.

"Thank God," I said to Corrie. "Maybe she'll make some friends."

Rashon did make friends. She made several, and she taught every one of them how to play hopscotch. They met in the mall, and they sang in chorus, or they rapped, but none of them had the staying power Rashon did, and when they had to go home, Rashon began singing to herself again.

"She is not a real human being," Corrie said.

We were watching the news.

"It won't last," I said. "You can't play hopscotch all day every day for your whole life."

Corrie shook her head. "She's been doing pretty well for the last five years."

"She's going to get bored one day. She's going to sit down on one of those benches and start getting pissed."

Corrie laughed. "She's already pissed."

"You think?"

"I know. Listen to the songs. A damn commentary..."

"There's my mother in the store, nobody talks to her no more." And: "Down on B there's a man and phone, ringrin-gring deliver it alone." Rashon sang what she saw, and her memory began to worry me. What she knew began to make me think she needed to start shutting up about some things.

ON HALLOWEEN, WE had a full moon. Corrie and I stayed in and watched TV. She didn't want to go out. She said there were enough freaks in the city on a normal day. I wanted to get out of the house and go to Cafe Iguana, but Corrie insisted Halloween wasn't the night to get drunk in Manhattan. We

turned off the lights and settled onto the couch to watch a
horror movie.

The community was holding a party for neighborhood kids
in the co-op building across the mall, and two men guarded
the entrance. The guards didn't let kids come and go. Once
you left the party, you were out of the party. Rashon, however,
never went inside. She entertained the guards with their own
personal song. In the midst of our movie, we heard her singing, "I'm a big man, I guard the door, once you leave, can't get
in no more."

Then we heard several voices.

"Probably got kicked out," Corrie said. She got up and
looked out the window. "We should watch this instead."

I walked over to the window and leaned on the window
sill. Boys crowded around the two guards, and they were big,
those teenagers.

"No alcohol," the guard said.

"We'll leave it out here, man."

"You can't go back in now, and you know it. Go on."

The guards herded the boys into the mall, and the little
clot of them lingered.

"Can't go in 'cause you got booze. Can't go in so you all
lose."

I saw a boy turn toward Rashon. I watched them gathering. I watched the flaming tips of their cigarettes, huddled

together like low-born stars, watched them walking through the steam seeping out from under the manholes, and I wanted Rashon to go inside.

I yelled, "Rashon, go inside now."

"Hey, fuck you," said a boy, and then the fuck you became a chorus, punctuated by whistles and laughter and the occasional *fuck me, baby*; and Rashon stood, shielding her eyes to help her to see, but our lights were off, and my voice could have been anyone's, from any window.

The boys walked up and down in front of the building, yelling *fuck you*, until other windows opened, and then I could hear them all, the *shut up, assholes*, the *go fuck yourselves*, and the words in Spanish that I didn't understand. And as neighbors leaned out their windows and waved the boys away, and as the boys strutted up and down the mall, softly, faintly, the sound of Rashon's sandals against the pavement rose into the air, and at one odd clear moment, the high note of her song.

A boy grabbed Rashon by the arm as she jumped from square to square. She scratched his face. She tried to rip his hair out. She kicked and kicked and kicked, and when the guard pulled them apart, she did not stop moving, could not stop, and the guard held her, loosely, until she wore herself out, and her movements slowed, and she sat. The guards took Rashon inside, but the boys stayed outside. They sat on the benches.

Corrie said, "You think you're going to help her, Jenny, calling out like that? That little girl doesn't need your help."

I didn't answer.

"She had the guards right there. The boys wouldn't have hassled her much, just razzed her more than anything," Corrie said.

"Somebody has to look out for her."

Corrie stared at me. "You need to look out for yourself." She paused. "You think you know it all, don't you?"

"What do you mean?"

"This neighborhood can take care of its own."

"I am part of this neighborhood," I said, but the loneliness came in a wash then.

I went into my room and closed the door and listened to the night grow, to the sirens accumulate, to the rap, and the salsa. I poked my head under the blinds and watched the cars inch down the avenue. I watched the figures emerge from nowhere, and I watched the cars leave, turning right onto 11th, the tail lights getting smaller and smaller.

THE DAY AFTER Halloween I didn't want to go home and face Corrie. I worked late. I was reading reviews, highlighting passages that would sound good on the quote page. My boss, Irwin, asked me why I was staying. Irwin had tousled gray hair, where he had hair, and half-glasses that sat squarely on his nose. I shrugged. I told him I was catching up, but after he left, I thought, why am I staying? What the hell is worth staying for? A nine-to-five job that pays squat?

By the time I got home, the sky was black. There was no one at the bus stop when I climbed off, but I didn't notice. I was thinking about Corrie, looking up at the co-op, counting the floors to see if our lights were on. And then there he was, right beside me, saying "Hey baby," hey baby being one word, his voice breezy and low.

He touched me lightly on the elbow and then he gripped my elbow hard and tried to steer me off the street, away from the bus stop, away from the mall, which had lights, down onto 10th, which did not. He smelled of liquor and of garbage, and as we passed the last few streetlights, I could see his face, pale and unshaven, long blond hair laced with dirt. He didn't look at me, and I looked away. The smell, his smell, like he'd never bathed in his life, and I thought: this is my life.

I was on tip-toes. I was on tip-toes heading for a dark street, and suddenly I picked up the pace and ran. He laughed, a deep, throaty laugh. He whooped, and I smelled the alcohol, and then I thought, "This will not happen to me." I turned fast and let him walk right into my knee. I wrenched my elbow from his grip and ran down the sidewalk and into the mall, listening for footsteps, waiting for them, but the footsteps I heard were not his. They were Rashon's.

I said as I passed by, "Get inside, Rashon."

She continued to play.

I pulled open the co-op door, holding it for Rashon, and stared back down the mall. I couldn't see the man. Rashon had a song going. I didn't listen to her.

I said, "Rashon, you better get inside. There's a guy out here who just grabbed me."

She kept singing.

"Rashon," I said, "Get inside. Do you hear me?"

Rashon sang louder.

"Rashon," I yelled, but she didn't stop. She raised her voice, and she tossed her stone, and I stood there, watching her, looking for the boy. She never looked at me. She kept her head down, and she belted out her song, and her words were plain and clear and hard, "I got friends and you're not one. You a white girl you better run."

I remember thinking what people would say about me. *Oh, yeah, that new white girl from the co-op. Is that where she lived? Yeah, that one. Lived with Corrie. You know Corrie? What happened to the new girl? Man, man, people like that should never move here, you know? They got no community here.* I let the co-op door swing closed.

Corrie nearly ran into me as I tried to get on the elevator. I stepped back, and she fell forward, and then we stared at each other.

"You yelled," she said. And then, "You're really late."

I smiled at her, a sad smile, a short one, and then bit my lip. My head felt heavy, and a headache lurked behind my eyes, and then I started shaking, like I was cold.

Corrie put her arm around me, then she slowly walked us over to the co-op door and pushed it open.

"Rashon," she said, and there was something in her voice that made even me look at her. Rashon stopped her game.

"What?"

"Do you want to come inside with us or do you want to go to your apartment?"

Corrie did not command, but her choice was a clear one.

"What if I don't want to come in?"

Corrie shrugged. "Your mom's going to call you in soon anyway. But if I were you, I'd haul my ass inside now. Jenny told you some guy just grabbed her. You gonna' stay outside or take care of yourself?"

Rashon swung her arms, and then she swung a leg, and then she turned and, looking back once over her shoulder, strolled slowly into the building.

"I don't see a man," she said. She held my gaze.

Upstairs, in the apartment, Corrie made me tea. She brought me a blanket and a pillow and said to lie down on the couch. I didn't drink the tea. I took one sip and then curled up under the blankets and closed my eyes.

"I don't know the rules," I said, and she didn't answer.

I CALLED MOM early the next morning, and Earl answered the phone. I paused. I tried to sound casual, light.

"Hi, Earl. Is my Mom there?"

"Yes," he said, "but she's still asleep. Do you want me to get her? I was just heading out the door."

Why, I thought, can I not talk? I imagined him on the other end of the line, biting his lip, maybe wiping the sweat off his forehead. He would be wearing one of his blue Volvo shirts with his name stitched in red on a little white oval patch.

"Jenny, are you okay?" Earl finally asked.

I nodded, and then I kept nodding, and then I started crying, and I heard Earl, saying over and over, "It's okay. It's okay. Just get the hell out of there, and come on home."

ON MY LAST night in New York, Corrie took me out for a farewell drink. We walked home from Chelsea, then strolled slowly down the mall, and I looked up, buzzed, at the way the lights seemed to give a day-like quality to the night.

"This is not the city for you," Corrie said.

"Nope." I laughed, and then I felt like I hadn't laughed in a long, long time. "You know, it's not so bad a place to live," I said.

I said it knowing that the short walk from the bus stop to the mall to the building could seem interminable. I said it knowing that farther away, hidden in the shadows one block down, the heroin dealers lurked by the pay phones and the pay phones rang, and then like horses out of the block, young boys raced by on bicycles, in the cover of darkness.

Corrie stopped and lit a cigarette. "Well," she said, "I'll always live here." She looked up at the co-op. "What will you do now?"

"I'll go home for a while, and then I'll leave again."

"Where will you go?"

I shrugged.

The sky was pitch, and the lights in all the buildings had a strange kind of beauty, and the heavy beat of rap, and the intermingling of the salsa, sounded warm to me, easy going, and I felt, finally, like I could leave. In the steam rising from the manholes, two children played a game, and they came in and out of the fog like ghosts, and under the dim school yard lights, the boys leaned together, smoking, and there was something tense in their quiet, but calm, very calm, and rising into the night, like the steam, came Rashon's newest song. "Got myself a brand new dress, now I am lookin' like all the rest" and we stopped before we went inside, and listened. "I'm lookin' fine when I go out, I'm lookin' fine when I go out." The rhythm of her sandals against the pavement gave her the beat, and Rashon kept to it, despite the distractions. She had on the same old clothes.

"How are you doing tonight, Rashon?"

"I'm fine."

"Are you going to be out here for a while?"

"Long as I like."

I eyed the boys in the school yard, and then farther over, on the far corner, the two little kids playing in the steam.

"Play well," I said.

I didn't want to think about kids outside, in this neighborhood at night, didn't want to think about how, so used to the darkness, they played in steam and sang songs and would soon, perhaps, lurk in that school yard, waiting, because everybody in this neighborhood waited, for anything, for everything, for life to happen, for the chase, the bust, the parade, the carnival, that first kiss, sips of beer, a stolen glance, because that was the tension in the air, always, like a whisper, *What next.*

I turned, and as I turned, Rashon began to sing, softly, almost in a whisper, her voice cracking slightly on the high notes. "White girl, let me tell you what's up. White girl, let me tell you." I watched her hop away into the shadows, and I knew what the difference between us was: Rashon already knew how to balance. She knew where she belonged. She knew how to keep both feet on the ground.

I slung my purse over my shoulder, and it bounced when I hopped behind her, but she didn't acknowledge me. She sang the next line, "You got to watch out 'cuz the men are mean," and she turned at the top, and I hopped onward, aiming for safety, for the chance to breathe, for the chance to turn things around somehow, turn myself around, just like Rashon.

EARL MET ME at the airport. He waited at the gate, a little bit to the side of the crowd, and when he saw me, he waved. He had made me a sign that said "Ms. Jennifer Nelson," and when I saw it, I felt a little pang. He had been alone for years, living quietly, without too many ripples, and when I saw my sign I knew he was going to ask my mother to marry him.

I smiled. "Where's Mom?" I asked.

Earl looked hurt. "She's waiting for you at Brenda's house. You're all going to have dinner together, and I thought I'd come on over after that and maybe we'd all go have dessert someplace."

Suddenly I saw us the way Earl saw us: the inseparable four, the women all seated around mom's dining room table on Sunday afternoons, cutting out coupons and finishing homework and paging through catalogs. It was a flash, gone almost as it dawned on me, but I knew what he must feel, that alienation, that knowing that you are two steps behind, that feeling of exclusion that is never intended, always implied, and hurts like hell.

"That sounds nice, Earl," I said.

He drove me home in his old '78 Volvo station wagon. I

hadn't ridden in a car for a long time. I stretched out my legs. I fingered the rough edges of my cardboard sign. This is who I am, I thought. I am twenty-three years old, and my name is Jenny Nelson.

Brenda lived far out, on the edge of the suburbs, almost to that last edge of farm land. She lived on a dirt road that ran between two fields. I wondered how her house would look from a distance, how the road would sound, what the cold would feel like, out there, with all that space to give it emphasis.

"Will you drop me off at the top of the road, Earl?"

"Sure," he said.

He didn't ask me why. I think he knew I needed to feel the ground under my feet, to take my time. I climbed out of the car and held the door open. The cold made me shiver.

"So we'll see you soon, right?"

"Sure thing," he said.

I closed the door and went around to the back to grab my bags, but Earl waved me off through the window and drove on, and the cold came into me, a deep chill that seemed to crawl through my clothes and take root in my bones, and I knew I was home.

The sky was gray, heavy, as if at any moment a long, steady snow would start. Snow was already packed down on the road, the brown color of the trees. I turned around as I walked and scanned the open space, noticed how the snow lined the tree branches, and then I looked ahead, to the long white house almost lost in the landscape.

Walking along the road into the crisp, chill night, I knew, finally, what I had been missing back in New York. What drove me home was what originally drove me away. Brenda's voice and my mother's, and my grandmother's, and mine. My community of women.

I yelled, "Hey, ladies." Then, a sudden spreading of light as the front door opened, and my mother running, wordlessly, out of the dusk in a flurry of footfall and the smell of lavender and my grandmother peering out into the darkness and Brenda, a shadow on the steps, slashing the light with her hand as she waved.

BROTHERS

I AM WAITING, STUCK in a damn hole, for my little brother, Ephraim. He wrote to say he'd be visiting for his October break, to get away from books and mid-terms and papers, to visit me in the woods for a few days and be a He-Man. I read between the lines; I know why he is coming. We've had our first snow. A dusting, but with the snow comes the cold, and with the cold, Ephraim.

I planned to meet Ephraim on the road tonight, by the sign pointing toward my house. He said he'd pull in some-time before dark. I wanted him to see me waving at him from my chair, welcoming him, a half mile by dirt road from my house on a chilblain kind of day, on a day when more snow will come.

I wheeled my way down the dirt road from my house,

headed for the main road. Jack followed me, got bored, then disappeared into the trees, tracking a scent. I commanded him to stick by me, but he learned long ago that I can't chase after him, so he doesn't listen to me anymore.

The wind had a bite to it, reached through my coat and sweater and hip bone. Leaves fell suddenly in showers, and when I stopped to rest, head tilted back to scan the white sky, leaves rained down. When I righted my head, my lap was full of Fall.

I bounced along the dirt road, singing the Hallelujah chorus, until I hit the curve, at which point I got stuck in a hole. Kind of a dirt road pot hole. Kind of a half hole, half rut. A wheel trap. My chair sank on one side. I stopped singing. I rocked myself back and forth. Then I swore. I said every swear word I know. Then finally I sat, tilted into the hole, beginning to ache from the effort of keeping upright, and screamed. But I was too stubborn to move. I wanted to look strong and independent, not to slide out of the chair and crawl away from the danger. Ephraim wants me to move home, back to the Twin Cities, back to paved roads, to parking spots near store entrances, and to buses specially equipped with ramps which would magically lift me aboard. Ephraim is not alone in his concern. My friends preach at me in their letters (thank God they can't call). They tell me I should live where there is pavement. I write back and tell them very, very nicely to go to hell.

Only my parents leave me alone.

Ephraim and I talked about logistics last June, when I packed up to head east from the Twin Cities. In the middle of his finals, he drove home from Northfield and packed boxes with me, each of us sitting on the kitchen floor, sorting my dishes from Ellen's, packing them in crumpled newspaper for protection. Then he loaded my truck for me, according to my sideline directions. When he was finished, we sat on the front lawn and drank beers.

He said then: "You can't live up there alone."

I said, "Who should I ask to join me? Ellen?"

He winced, shook his head no. "You need a companion."

"The doctor said I should be fine alone."

"Should."

"Will be."

"Easy for him. He's not going to be the one worrying, is he?"

The next day, he drove me here. I imagine he thought, they all thought, that a summer here would be all I'd need.

Eph is a psychology major at Carleton. He thinks he understands me better than I understand myself. He lectures me by mail. Get counseling. Join a support group. The accident is too recent a development in your life, he scribbles, you need help. I love my brother, but the colder the weather becomes, and the longer I stay in the cabin, the more prescriptive and urgent his letters become, and the more his letters begin to piss me off.

I was 8 when Ephraim was born. At that age, I wasn't too impressed with him. What was so special about a baby? Not that I didn't care about him, but at that age I was interested mostly in, well, myself. My life then consisted of one-on-one basketball with Timmy Murphy, who constantly kicked my ass, and swimming lessons at the U. My major concern was catching the bus; my greatest joy, snowball fights after a fresh snowfall. But I wasn't a complete bastard. Once Eph started to talk, once he sounded human, I tried to be a good big brother. He needed a big brother. Ephraim was scrawny. A shock of black hair hung in his eyes. Big, blue eyes like spheres. Knobby knees. Elbows covered with Band-Aids. Untied shoe laces.

When the neighborhood kids gathered together at our house for games of Kick the Can or Capture the Flag, I made sure Eph played. Our yard was the biggest, and we would meet, after dinner but before dark, by the rhododendron bushes stretching along the front of our house. The Murphys, the Andersons, the Franklins, and us. Whatever team I got picked for also got Eph, even if he was too little to understand the rules. We were a package.

And once, when all the other kids were running around, tagging each other, squealing, little scrawny Ephraim, whom everybody ignored, jogged straight across the front yard into the rhododendron bushes and emerged with the flag. Which, by the way, he did not wave in the air in victory but brought to me.

This is Ephraim now: thick, black glasses, as if he chose them on purpose, to accentuate his paleness and the sharp edges of his nose and jaw. Thin build. Shock of black hair falling in his eyes. In his thin, almost anorectic face, his eyes dominate.

But I'm getting sidetracked. Point is, Ephraim is coming to visit the family cabin, now converted into my home.

I live deep in the woods in western Wisconsin, like a Thoreau wanna-be. I'm not far from Amery, but my back yard is a forest; my front, Lake Divine. I live simply. I work with my hands. Carpentry. I earn my living by making furniture. My hands are all I have, chilblains, calluses, and all.

This is my life: ranch style house with a front porch (equipped with hand-crafted porch swing); weather-beaten dock; *Yankee Magazine* subscriptions; herb and vegetable garden; a rusting Ford pick-up; and a yellow lab named Jack, who has a bit of a farting problem. I'm constantly opening the front door and ushering Jack outside, which is, in the end (no pun intended), pointless. I'm still left with the stink, and I'd rather have his company.

We have seasonal rituals, Jack and I, developed over the last four years, long before we moved here last June. At first we used to spend weekends at the cabin with Ellen, because she wouldn't stay any longer than two days. Then last year we began to spend weekends alone while she stayed home in Minneapolis and worked. I packed my Ford on Friday nights;

she typed her thesis from longhand notes. I fished; she ran her experiments a third and fourth time.

We were graduate students together at the University of Minnesota, in Dr. Whitman's cell bio lab. We used DNA technology to study basic biological questions about sperm, a constant source of amusement to my family and friends. *How are those sperm studies with Ellen coming?* And on and on.

Unlike me, she will finish her thesis, earn her Ph.D., become a Dr., Dr. Johnson. She will teach. She will run experiments, write papers, perhaps discover something important about male fertility. I will discover nothing about male fertility.

Last fall, Jack and I escaped weekend after weekend, then for week after week, ignoring my thesis altogether. Teaching? Research? Suddenly, after four years in a Ph.D. program, I dropped the ball. Lost interest. Doubted. I re-read *Walden* once too often.

These are Jack's and my rituals:

In fall I paddle the canoe, with Jack sitting in the middle like an emperor, into the marshes and listen to the birds' mating calls. Chickadee, Redwing Blackbird. We watch geese fly into a V, then point across the sky. Sometimes Jack maneuvers himself so that his front paws rest on the seat. Then he barks. When the birds dart away, he is satisfied. Usually.

Ephraim would die if he knew I still canoed. Suddenly, for the first time in my life, I have secrets from him. I could explain how I canoe, how I wheel myself down to the dock, slide out of my chair, scoot near the edge, and lift my legs inside the canoe; how I slide my ass into the boat and up onto the seat. How I wear a life jacket. How I make Jack sit still. I could explain all this, but Ephraim would worry.

In winter Jack watches while I pour maple syrup over snow. We eat homemade soup. And if the main road is passable, the Sunday before Christmas we drive the two miles to the Lundberg's house and sing carols to them. Or at least, I sing. Jack farts along in time, or at least he farts enough that he could be a metronome. Then old Mr. Lundberg fires up his Volvo. Mrs. Lundberg wraps a scarf around her head, carries her hot dish in her arms, reminds Mr. Lundberg to watch out for ice, and off we go.

Houses, some of which are dark, cob-webby, and dank for half the year, line the lake. We bypass these houses and move in a slow caravan around the lake, picking up household by household, until we arrive back at my house, where we eat together. One family provides the ham, another the rolls, and so on. Only eleven people live on Lake Divine year round. Now with me, this year we'll be twelve. We are a small band.

But this year I won't sing at the Lundberg's doorstep. I'll be here, waiting for them all to arrive.

On summer nights Jack and I watch smoke plumes rise through the trees, a hundred signal fires from a hundred sacrifices to the gods. Campfires of people with power boats and L.L. Bean hiking boots and Gore-Tex sleeping bags. We nailed small signs to the trees at our property line. The signs read: Come up this path and incur our wrath. Only one man has ever come up the path, and when he did, God help me, he asked if he might use the toilet. I asked him what the hell he was doing away from home if he couldn't just pee in the woods. He was a travel writer.

We rarely have visitors, which is the point of living up here. Getting away, escaping. This is what Ephraim fails to understand, that I want to be alone, that the solitude is healing.

I shiver, then rock my chair from side to side. Ephraim will be here soon. Makes a person think quite a bit, being stuck in a hole, just before a snowfall, on a blind curve. I wonder if I should swallow my pride, fall out of the chair, and drag myself home. I have done this before.

Last April, I dragged myself across Ellen's and my front yard in a desperate attempt to get my own morning paper. I was fresh out of the hospital, fresh out of therapy, and I was going to get the piece of shit thing myself. Ellen stood on the front steps, her arms folded across her chest, auburn hair loose around her shoulders, and watched as I pulled myself across the lawn to the sidewalk and back. Maybe it was asking too much, to let her see me like that, to see the desperation, and the pain.

But I knew before that April morning that she would leave me. I knew in late January. We were sitting in my room in the University of Minnesota hospital. Where my advisor visited me, as did my fellow grad students, and even the Head of the Department. The beds in my room had metal frames, adjustable like the ones advertised on TV, and the floor was easy to clean tile. Sun slipped through the window. Outside, traces of snow covered the ground. Mild winter, balmy for Minnesota. Ellen wore one of my flannel shirts.

We had the room to ourselves. The day was a Sunday, a day we once spent in bed reading *The New York Times*. Sipping coffee. Eating omelets. Avoiding discussions of work, how my experiments were going, whether or not she'd written any more of her thesis. We hadn't shared Sundays like that for a while. I was at the cabin, she was at the lab. My thesis was stalled, but hers was not. For me, each page was tedious to write. Before my accident, my advisor had written me a warning note, stating that my progress, or lack thereof, was unsatisfactory.

She came to the hospital directly from the lab. Her hair was pulled back into a ponytail. She sat in front of the window, looked out. I stared at her face in profile, at a stray curl of auburn hair which followed the line of her cheekbone, at her long, thin nose, at her slightly parted lips. When she took off her glasses, leaned her head back and stretched, the gesture made me ache.

We talked about nothing. Chatted. Chatting with Ellen

killed me. I needed her to know one thing. I needed her to know I planned to move to the cabin. Dad had said to me, Take it, George, if you want it, the cabin is yours. I realized, looking at her avoid looking at me, that I always imagined myself living there alone.

I said, "I'm thinking of going to live at the cabin."

"You've just hit a saturation point," she replied.

"No, I haven't hit a saturation point," I said.

At first, I thought she hadn't heard me. She continued to stare out the window, as if transfixed. I repeated myself. Ellen turned from the window, put her glasses back on.

"You'll finish, despite all..." she waved her hand in the air, "despite this."

"I don't think I'll ever finish my thesis," I said.

Ellen's eyes met mine. "Why?"

For a moment, I was silent. "Because I don't care anymore," I said.

She turned back to the window without saying a word. I missed her then, I missed her already, though she took until April, until shortly after the paper episode on the front lawn, to tell me we were over. Four years, instantly reduced to the past tense, within the span of a brief conversation.

This is a frightening concept, the end of romantic love. Numbing.

Sounds good, saying shattered sacroiliam, crushed femurs.

Spahenous. Tibular. Ishiatic. But what do the terms mean? Couch the damage in technical language. Don't translate.

I will not walk again.

I will not make love again.

I am 28 years old.

And I am sitting in the middle of the dirt road which leads from my house to the main road, stuck in a goddamn hole.

I scream again, and again, and Jack returns, barking. He licks my hand. He talks to me. He shakes. I shake.

A sick feeling grips me. I envision Ephraim barreling around the curve in his used Honda Civic wagon, driving straight into me. I have an aversion to vehicles. I have nightmares. In this case, the psychology is simple.

I fell asleep at the wheel after a late night at the lab. I ran a red light at Hennepin and Excelsior and drove into a pit. The station wagon went front end first off the road, off the sidewalk, and down, at 45 mph. I hit my head. I now have a thin white scar on my temple and cheek. The tug of the seat belt broke my collar bone. I broke my back.

Now I am in a war with my health insurance. Negligence. They're suing me for falling asleep, suing me to prevent paying my claim.

I sit in my hole and think about what I will do if they won't pay.

The sky is darkening.

Finally I lean to fall forward, but I hear tires crunching in the dirt. I yell. Jack barks. I wave my arms into the headlights, I scream frantically. Glare of yellow lights, wheels spitting dirt, and though the sounds are not the same sounds, I remember. The pressure, no pain. No pain, just pressure. Voices swirling above my head. Saws whirring, cutting into metal. Thinking. I was thinking as I listened to the voices and the saws, I've crashed, but I don't feel any pain, so I must be okay. I must be okay.

I feel a hand on my shoulder, but I can't look up.

"You okay, George?"

I nod, unable to speak. Finally, I look at my brother. His eyes are large behind his thick glasses, and his hair, as usual, is falling in his eyes. He is wearing a purple, knit Minnesota Vikings cap. The hat covers his ears.

"Are you okay? What the hell are you doing in the middle of the road?"

"I'm stuck."

"Stuck?"

"In a hole."

Nervous laugh. "Good thing I'm here, huh?"

Ephraim pushes against me three times before I even budge. I'm not a small man; I am not slight like he is.

"Why did you ever move here, George? I don't...get...it. Are you going to help me or are you just going to sit there?

You could lean forward or something. Shit."

When he pushes, I rock forward, but to no avail. Finally Ephraim hauls me out of my chair, sets me on the dirt, and tugs at my chair. The wheel sticks. He works the wheel loose. I watch sweat bead on his forehead. I say nothing.

"You look the same except for the Rip Van Winkle beard," he says, stepping back to give me a once over. He smiles a thin smile, hauls me into his Honda, grabs an old towel from the trunk to wipe the mud of my wheels, then carefully places the chair in the back seat. Jack jumps into the back seat and squirms to find a comfortable position away from my chair. We drive to the cabin.

"Good to see you," I say.

"You, too."

We are silent until I shiver.

"Getting cold up here," Ephraim says.

I know what's coming, so I look out my window.

"I think you should consider moving back into the Cities," he says as we approach the cabin.

"How's school?" I ask.

"Don't avoid the subject, George."

"I'm not interested in moving back, Eph."

"You're not safe up here alone."

I shrug.

He leans forward on the wheel, even though he has his

lights on high beam. I can't remember if he has always driven like this or not. My memories are selective.

In the hospital immediately after the accident, I lay in a hard bed, with a curtain pulled around me to provide the illusion of privacy, and the nurses, who smelled like cleaning detergent, wiped my ass. I touched my thighs constantly, my calves, my toes, unable to comprehend touch without sensation. Sometimes, I'd forget who I was and get up to go to the bathroom. Or try. I'd sit up, feel resistance, a weight, remember, lie back down. At night, when I am groggy and disoriented, I continue to make this mistake.

When we reach the house, it is dark. The air is clear, crisp, and the moon is hidden in the night sky. Snowflakes fall. Ephraim unloads my chair, helps me into it, pushes me up the ramp onto my porch.

The cabin is cool. I wheel myself to the fireplace.

"How about a fire?" I ask.

"Sounds great."

His only luggage is his Carleton backpack. He dumps the backpack on the couch. The couch is a pull-out. He will sleep on it tonight, in front of the fire. My house is small. Two bedrooms, one of which I converted into a workshop. Bathroom. Living room with fireplace. Kitchen. At our pre-Christmas pot-lucks, we are snug.

Jack sits beside me as I stuff twigs into the fireplace, light them, blow. Together we watch the fire catch. I drop logs onto the flames, grunting because they are heavy. Eph bends to assist me, but I brush him off. I can do this. I make fires all the time. I crumple up the Lake Divine Gazette, which Mrs. Lundberg edits, if edit is the word. Every week we twelve Lake Divine residents receive, among other tidbits, a new recipe. This week's recipe is for brisket.

I let the newspaper catch. Then: "Drink?"

Eph laughs. "Are you kidding? This is October break. Give me the bottle."

Ephraim sits in front of the fire, on the floor, and Jack creeps over to him. Ephraim strokes his fur. I wheel myself into the kitchen.

"How're classes?" I ask.

"Pretty hard this semester. I'm glad for the break. I have a history class which is hell. The history of Russia. On our reading list for the first week of classes, the teacher assigned <u>War and Peace</u> as optional, recommended reading. I'm not kidding. Can you believe it?"

"Who's teaching?"

"Atwater. I don't think she was teaching when you were there."

I mix Eph a screwdriver, though he hasn't specifically asked for one. When I hand him the drink, he chuckles.

"Wheee," he says, raising his glass to meet mine.

"To passing history," I say.

"Amen."

We sit in front of the fire, him in the lounge chair, me in my metal one, Jack now stretched out between us on the floor. The night is quiet. The fire snaps, eats up Mrs. Lundberg's brisket recipe. I wonder now if I'll regret losing that recipe, since winter is coming.

I make us a second round. Then a third. Most of the time we sit silently. Ephraim laughs each time Jack farts. Ephraim laughs frequently.

We switch to whiskey. We drink too much, and Ephraim begins harping on me again. "Move back to the Cities," he says.

"No."

"Why?"

"I want to be alone."

"You're withdrawing."

"No," I answer emphatically. "I just don't want to live that way."

"What way?"

"With the noise. With crowds. With deadlines. I want a simple life. I want...to live simply."

Eph sinks back into his chair." It's Ellen, isn't it?"

I shake my head no.

Eph is staring into the fire, slumped down into the chair, and his legs stick straight out. He looks like how I feel sometimes, when moving myself into a chair is too much effort, when I rest with my legs left wherever they fall.

"No, I guess it's not Ellen," he says. And then: "It's everything. Everything is shoving you away, making you want to be a hermit."

I nod. "I want to be a hermit."

"George-..."

I cut him off. I'm tired. I'm fed up. I want to pace, but I can't. I want to run around Lake Divine, but I can't. And I want to be alone, and I will be.

"Eph, don't push me. I'm fine. Sally Anderson brings my groceries once a month. Amery is what, half an hour away at most? I have my dog. I have my view."

"What if it snows twenty inches? You'll be trapped."

"Lundberg will bail me out."

"He's almost seventy five." Ephraim throws his hands up in the air. "For God's sake, George, I found you stuck in a hole. A hole. Come home. How much more clearly can I say it?"

"Mom and Dad are fine with me being up here, Eph, so don't stress it."

"Mom and Dad are worried sick. They just won't tell you."

I finish my drink. I wonder how many I've had. I don't care. Jack smiles at me and whines. His tail thumps against the hard wood floor. I reach down and scratch behind his ears. He is the constant in my life. He does not change. At first, he growled at my chair. Now he is used to the wheels.

The fire is dying, and we let it die.

I wheel myself into the kitchen, make another drink.

"Don't you think you've had enough, George?"

"Ephraim, why don't you lay off?"

"I'm trying to help."

"Well, all you've succeeded in doing is pissing me off. In fact, all you've done for months is piss me off. Through the mail, no less."

"Come home."

"Lay off."

"Oh, for God's sake, George, what the hell do you think is going on? You're paralyzed. Why don't you say it? Can't you say it? What the hell are you trying to prove?"

"I'm not coming home. This is my home. If you don't think it's safe, if you don't like it, tough shit. Leave."

He stares at me.

"Leave." I point to the door.

Jack comes into the kitchen. He talks to me. He paws at my legs.

Ephraim tilts his head to the side, blinks, then stands. He slides into his coat, digs in his pocket, then pulls out his keys. He looks at them, then puts them back into his pocket.

"I'm going for a walk."

The front door slams. My head is circling. I close my eyes.

Jack paws at my leg, and lazily I pat his head. Then I wheel myself to the door, try to put on my coat but the thing gets twisted. Finally, I get the damn thing on, wheel outside, roll down my mini-ramp. Jack darts ahead, snapping at snow-flakes.

"Eph?"

Ephraim will not look at me. His head is thrown back, his mouth is open to swallow snow.

"Ephraim."

He begins walking, and I follow him, still calling his name. He waves me away. He picks up his pace, then jogs, then runs. I follow, but my progress is slow. He rounds the curve and disappears. I roll forward, one more push, stare hard at the ground, searching to avoid the hole, then let my arms fall to my sides. Too dark to see.

I shiver. Snow melts on my bare head.

"Ephraim," I whisper.

I live a quiet life. Deep in the woods. Simple. Keep my life simple.

I will not let myself turn and go back down the dirt road alone.

I push hard against the wheels, press forward. My chair sinks on one side. Fuck. This time I will not sit and scream. I command Jack to sit and magically, he does, though he whines at me.

I slide from my chair carefully. The ground is wet and cold. I trace the shape of my chair, of the wheel that is lodged in the rut, and I tug hard at the rubber. I dig at the earth, then slide around to the back of my chair and pull on the wheels. The wheel does not give. I dig at the earth with my bare hands. Pull, inch backward, pull, inch backward, until the chair pops free. I drag myself around to the front of my chair and pull my wet, muddy body into the seat. Leaves stick to me.

There is only so far I can go, only so far I can follow.

I am numb. I have had too much to drink. I have not drunk enough.

Ephraim will get cold and come back soon. And I'll wait for him by the fire with Jack, in my house. I'll wait for my brother, and when he walks through the door, I'll hand him a towel and a cup of coffee. I'll let him sit for a minute. I'll tell him I'll get a phone line. And then I'll say, as kindly as I can, that I can't leave my home, that I can't go back.

PATCHWORK

I FOUND IT WHEN I was cleaning out my grandmother's cedar chest, a small lock of hair, one curl, tucked into the pages of John's first epistle. I'd been looking for a bundle of old newspapers that my grandmother wanted me to see, but once I discovered the hair, I forgot about the papers. I knew whose hair this was. I recognized the yellow, almost golden color, my grandmother had once described. It was Cecily's hair. Cecily, whose name had long ago been erased from the family tree.

The cedar chest stood in what was once my grandparents' bedroom. For most of my life, they had lived on the lower level of my parents' house, in three adjoining rooms. I used to sit on their shag carpet floor and watch television or hold my grandmother's hand and talk, each of us sunk into their old striped couch, shoulders touching. I thought I'd seen everything they owned in the long years of growing up. I thought, during the days we packed Grandma and Grandpa for the nursing home, I'd seen everything in the cedar chest.

I put the lid of the cedar chest down. A thin layer of dust lined the top, like the new, thin layer of silence that had filled the house since Grandma and Grandpa had left; like the old layer of silence, long undisturbed, that I had just discovered.

Cecily. Spitfire. Flame. Turner. "She turned," Grandma had said once, "like milk."

GRANDMA WAS WAITING for me in the nursing home lobby. She sat on the blue flowered couch, feet crossed at her ankles, hands folded. She stared at the floor, and she didn't move unless she saw a blur of feet pass by, then she squinted at the passing shape. Her hair, newly permed and carefully arranged, covered her growing bald spot. She looked thin, and the wheelchair placed strategically within reach was a sure sign that she was feeling weak today, unable to use her walker. Yet when she took my hand, her grip was strong.

"Did you find them?" she asked. There was a story behind the newspapers that she wanted to tell me so that I could include it in the family history we were compiling.

"No, but I found something else I want to talk about."

I pulled a plastic baggy from my purse and laid it gently in Grandma's hands. Grandma pressed the plastic flat to see, then pulled the hair out and ran it between her fingers.

"I was surprised to find this," I said.

Grandma squinted at the hair, bent over it.

"I'd like to write about *her*," I said.

"No, not her."

"But she's-"

"She's nothing," Grandma said. She closed her hand around the curl of hair, tugged at her wheelchair with the other. "Cecily is not family."

I avoided her gaze. In the lobby, the other scattered stuffed chairs were empty. Grandma swatted at my hand.

"Push me to the window," she said. "I'll watch you leave."

Surprised, I took her by the arm, lowered her gently into the wheelchair. Grandma still had Cecily's hair, and I worried about what she would do with it, maybe flush it, but I didn't have the courage to ask. I pushed her to the window.

"I love you," I said, uncertain what my sudden dismissal might mean.

She tilted her head up to look at me and smiled. "Leave Cecily out," she said.

I gave her a kiss on the cheek and said nothing. I waited for the doors to open, marched out into the frigid air. It was late January, cold enough in Minnesota that I should have hurried to my car. Instead, I turned and looked back at her. She was holding that curl of hair up to the light.

CECILY MANNING MORRIS Huffner Bowes. The fifth of nine children, squashed between Jocelyn and Edward, both of whom died of diphtheria. Born in 1909, died in 1953. Left no will.

"That," my grandmother once said, "is a crock. She left plenty of will behind, just not the kind they were looking for."

Grandma talked about Cecily on rare occasions, on days when I traipsed home from school in thick snow, and dark came early, and we sat at the kitchen table reviewing the day. Maybe after a glass of wine, when Grandpa started telling stories, and Grandma would insist he had them wrong, and the stories got lost temporarily in the debate. Sometimes then, amidst the chaos, Cecily came through in a line.

I knew that Cecily had sinned, but I didn't know what could drive her apart from the family, make her what she had become, a whisper, a sideways glance, an interrupted line, never recovered. Didn't she deserve a sentence or two in the family history? Everyone got at least a line. Each lady also got a square.

In my parents' basement, packed carefully into cardboard boxes with the baby clothes my mother hopes to pass on, is the women's patchwork quilt. Each generation adds a row, or at least a square. My grandmother's square is now pale yellow. It's plain save for the careful red stitching that makes her name. Catherine Andersen.

The plainness of her square is striking in a patchwork quilt of names and symbols, favorite colors and long quotes. Whitman. Roosevelt. The Bible. Her name is all she needed to record. *I was here*, it seems to say, *once a long time ago, and I was called Catherine.*

I am Sarah, and I will not sew my name for years. I won't sew my name until I know who I am, can script with such confidence the identity I struggle to define, until I know, as easily, and with such simplicity, the way to be remembered.

Cecily knew. In the second to last row of the quilt is her square, all her names in succession, each one stitched in a different color.

How she had added hers, I'll never know. By the time she had accumulated all those names, she was already persona non grata. But if anyone could get something done, it had to be Cecily.

Cecily, I was told, flipped her long, gold hair once too often. Cecily liked to watch football games with Grandpa, smoking cigarettes one after the other. She went through men just as fast, Grandma said. Cecily used to waltz into Grandma's house, swinging that hair, swinging those slim little hips. She had all the curves in all the right places and liked to show them off, to twist around on the sidewalk to see who might be watching her, to sashay into one of Grandpa's card games or football parties and take a seat.

After all the buildup, I'd expected more. A bank robber, a witch. But what I got was a sassy woman who had had no luck in love. Nothing about Cecily seemed shocking. After all, I lived with my boyfriend, Al. I didn't think she should have been run out of the family will, erased from the family tree. I thought she deserved a round of applause for persistence. And though I wasn't supposed to, I surreptitiously began to write Cecily into the family stories, giving her entire sections all her own because no one, it seemed, would share a story with her.

AT FIRST, WRITING the family stories was a blessing. Writing them down gave me a break from the endless, seemingly hopeless, task of e-mailing resumes and calling contacts. *Hello, I'm Sarah MacMillan, and I recently left Pillsbury. Chose to leave Pillsbury. Told my boss he was irresponsible and stormed out the door of Pillsbury. Punched the doughboy and ran. Hello, I'm Sarah MacMillan, and my savings are almost gone.* The family stories became a lifeline, something else for me to think about, something more for Grandma than routine.

I'd looked for work the first week of January, but in the second, I pushed away my draft resumes and picked up a pen. The words came easily, like water, and I turned the page. I wrote one morning, then the next, and my job search slipped quietly into its own dark grave. I didn't ask myself why I was writing, or for whom, or for how long. I simply let the pages fill. I ate Cap'n Crunch. I paced the house with my cat, Alber, in step, and together we etched the family history into something tangible. We wrote it down, each step a story, each story a life.

Grandma spent hours with my first stories. She settled in the lobby by the largest window she could find. She held each page in one hand, out to the light like a gift, and slowly passed her heavy magnifying glass over each word. Grandma asked for larger type, and I returned with the font so large that I felt like I'd written things on a billboard. For days, Grandma read as if possessed. The speed with which she read, for a woman who is legally blind, should have warned me. It didn't.

"The Cartwright women did not have big fannies," Grandma said, after finishing the first stories.

As a descendant of the Cartwrights herself, I thought this was going to be hard to contest.

"We have round fannies," she said. "Not big. Round."

This was her single comment.

Every story had five versions. She wanted hers.

AFTER GRANDMA'S REACTION to my first stories, I drove out to see Mom. January was slipping past, February loomed, and Grandma wanted more stories. I only had part of Cecily's. I needed advice.

Cecily wasn't easy to write about. The pictures of her that remained were few, black and white, and hard to see. Beautiful wavy hair, long. She was almost always smiling, almost always smoking. Her handwriting, in the few letters Grandma had saved, was thin, tight and scrunched. "Dear Cath," her early letters began. And then a later one, written from St. Louis late in 1948, which began, "Catherine." Other than the quilt, the curl, and the photos, that was all of Cecily that remained.

Mom met me at the door in jeans and a maroon sweater, long hair pulled back in a braid, her gray streak twisting down her back. At the old yellow kitchen table, bare in spots where the paint had chipped, my mother finished the sentences Grandma used to break off.

When Mom was little, Cecily had swept through the door one night like she belonged, grabbed a bottle of beer from the refrigerator, and walked into the living room. Mom had followed her, lingering in the door, waiting for her hello. Cecily said nothing to Mom or Grandma, but she said a hello to each of the men in turn. Hello, Sammy. Joe. Ed. Then she took her seat at the card table, on Grandpa's lap.

Grandpa tried to laugh her off. The other men laughed, too, and Mom laughed. Grandma didn't. She marched into the living room with a bowl of peanuts and set the bowl down hard. Cecily stayed right where she was, sipping her beer, laughing. Grandma offered Cecily a chair, and Cecily said no thanks, she didn't need one. Grandpa tried to shoo her off. There was a silence then. One of the other men coughed; another lit a cigarette, and Mom remembered that cigarette, the way the tip glowed when the man sucked in, the way the air seemed to fill, suddenly, with the smell. Then Grandpa pushed so hard, Mom said, that Cecily fell.

Twice more Cecily tried to settle where she should not have settled, at least twice more that Mom knew. The last time, Mom woke to Grandma yelling. She walked into the kitchen. Grandma had Cecily by the hair, and Grandpa was trying to pull them apart. Grandma wouldn't let go.

"Did they have an affair?" I asked.

"He was so handsome," Mom said. "He really was. You've seen the pictures. He had that confidence that comes with good looks. He walked tall. He laughed easily. To Cecily, I think, he was the one. But he wouldn't have acted on it. She embarrassed him. I think he was truly ashamed of her."

"Was Cecily crazy?"

"Maybe. What sane person does that?"

"Were there other letters, after 1948?"

Mom nodded. "She wrote for the rest of her life, but Grandma threw the letters out."

"Why not tell me all this?"

My mother smiled. "Really? You know your grandmother.

She asked me not to, and it seemed okay to me, not to carry that particular ghost through the generations."

There are turning points, turns of fortune, turns like Cecily's, when the heart withers and the spirit sours. Suddenly my vision of the family changed. We were not as strong or as solid as I'd thought. We were not a fortress. We never had been. We'd only ever been human, individuals whose foibles were magnified by size.

"Then why does she have a square in the quilt?" I asked.

"Think about the difference between a quilt and a history," my mother said as I left. "The quilt makes it look like Cecily married all those men."

I TIMED MY next visit to the nursing home carefully, spotted Grandma in her current events lecture, and sneaked down the hall to Grandpa. He was sitting in bed, gray hair combed away from his forehead, Twins cap on. He was contemplating a chess board.

"What is that?" he asked, pointing at the black king. His hand shook. His finger, knotted with arthritis, curled like a talon.

"It's the king," I yelled.

"Oh," Grandpa said, not hearing.

I lifted the piece, put it into his palm, and rolled it around. "King," I said again, this time into his ear.

"I'm losing against myself." He said, then he laughed. "King," he said and nodded.

"I want to talk to you," I said, and Grandpa, magically, turned his head toward me. "About Cecily."

He set the king down. "Move it someplace good for me. Don't tell me where."

"Cecily," I said again, placing the king in a free square, having no idea what the rules of chess allowed.

Grandpa sniffed. He was still looking at his chess board. He squinted, looking for the king. "Can't do that," he said, pointing to it.

I sighed, handed back the piece. Not even he would talk about her.

"She rooted for the Packers," Grandpa said, "just to be contrary." He held his elbow to steady his arm and plopped the king down on an appropriate square. The board shook. "She was a party girl. You know the type." Grandpa scrunched up his nose. "Nobody likes a girl like that. Why do you want to know about her?"

"Nobody liked her," I said, trying to keep my words at a minimum. The fewer my words, the better chance he had of hearing me.

"Nobody liked her," he agreed. "Except your grandmother." He laughed. "They were always close, those two. She'd never tell you that, but it was true. Grandma defended

Cecily, but the rest of the family. Well." Grandpa laughed. "Your grandmother never forgave Cecily."

"Never forgave her for what?"

"Sarah," he said, "she was a hussy." He sounded sad, as though he wished Cecily hadn't been.

"Did you like her?" I asked.

Grandpa didn't respond. He leaned back and rubbed his eyes. "When I play with your Al, he beats me every damn time," he said. " 'Course he can see. Makes a difference."

"Did you like Cecily, Grandpa?" I asked, tapping his arm, making him look at me.

Grandpa stared at me blankly. He knew, must have known, what I was asking. "She was a hard girl to like," he said.

Grandpa readjusted his hat, and I brushed an imaginary hair off his shoulder, just to touch him.

"Tell your Al to sneak in some scotch," Grandpa said as I left. He patted me on the back, winked, gave me the OK sign with his fingers. "Maybe if he gets drunk, he'll lose."

I stopped to look at Grandma in current events. She was sitting in the front row, directly in front of the speaker.

"You do not abandon family," Grandma had often said during my growing up years, "no matter what."

But Cecily had abandoned family every time she appeared at a card game. Later she bought a one-way bus ticket to St. Louis. It wasn't until I talked to Mom that I understood. All the names Cecily took were never hers, just the name of the man of the moment. She was all these and more.

"She was too free," Grandma had said on one of those rare winter evenings, when she forgot she didn't want to remember.

But that wasn't true. Cecily wasn't free. She had exacted a price. She nearly cost Grandpa a marriage, and she cost herself a family.

AT THE END of January, Kirsten, my grandparents' day nurse, had taken to calling me with any problems, since I was the family member most easily reached.

"I'm busy looking for work," I'd said the first day she'd called, the day I had gotten up at my normal time, dressed for success in my pajamas, and stayed in bed while Al trundled off to teach. Kirsten had ignored me, which was probably just as well.

Soon, though, she began to command me. I better do this, and I better do that.

"You better get over here," she said after I had dropped off new stories for Grandma, including Cecily's. "Your grandmother has a few words for you."

"I can't come over until later."

Kirsten took a deep breath. She said, "I am not living with this all day."

That cemented it.

"I'll be there at eight," I said. "p.m."

Grandma was furious when I arrived. She sat on the blue couch in the lobby and watched who came, who went. She wore her best sweat suit, a teal blue. In her lap lay the family history, the pages neatly tied around the middle with rubber bands.

"You've been avoiding me," she said the minute I swept through the door and she recognized my blur.

"I have not been avoiding you."

"Yes, you have. Kirsten called you this morning. I know. I was sitting *right there*." She punctuated her sentence with jabs in the air.

I sat down in an overstuffed chair opposite the couch. My grandmother squinted at me, and my heart beat faster.

"You wrote about Cecily." She pulled out a sheaf of pages and handed them to me.

"What are you doing?"

"Taking her back out."

I saw the way this could go, the bitterness, the awful words that could fly between us and never be recovered. I had only described Cecily's childhood, and then Manning; the absence of the marriage everyone expected, and the sudden, unexpected appearance of Morris. A ticket to St. Louis and then nothing. I had let Cecily whisk herself away.

I said, "What do you want to do, write her out after 1948?"

And that was where we left the entire family history, right

where it was, in 1948, the year Cecily left as well, calling herself Cecily Morris.

"I don't want you to change it when I'm gone," Grandma said, voice trembling.

"I would never do that."

"You said you would never write about Cecily either, but you did," Grandma snapped.

"I won't change the history," I said.

"You think you know what it was like to have a sister like her back then?" Grandma pursed her lips. "Well, you don't."

"I have an idea. I talked to Grandpa. And Mom."

Grandma stiffened. "That was my business to tell."

"What does it matter?"

"It matters to me. I don't want that known. Do you understand?"

"You, who said never to abandon family."

Grandma stood up slowly, gripping her walker. She lifted her chin. She said, "I am the vine and my Father is the gardener. He cuts off every branch in me that bears no fruit, while every branch that does bear fruit he trims clean so that it can be even more fruitful. John 15."

I knew we had come to a new place, she and I. I had Cecily's pages in my hand, and I grabbed my coat. I, too, stood. "Anyone who claims to be in the light but hates his brother is still in the darkness. John's first epistle."

"Get out."

I blazed out the door.

"You cannot write what you want. It's not just your story."
Her voice had a strength then that I had not heard for weeks,
a power that made it rise and crack.

Who could lay claim to the past? That was what we were
arguing about, who would control the way we were remembered. We had not thought of what we were doing. We had
not practiced the kinds of verbal reconciliation that we'd need.
That came later, slowly, like the snow that winter.

FEBRUARY ROLLED IN with a storm. The snow came, and
it hung in the air like a bad mood. Grandma and I settled
into our fight, as stubborn as the cold, as unwilling to budge.
Each day, Al carved a path from the back door to the sidewalk, and each day the snow covered it. Each day, I waited for
Grandma to call, and she for me, and so we sat, miles apart,
stories away, fuming over what was only ever ours to share.
The snow trickled down, settling like dust.

I recognized then, in the hushed world of the snowstorm,
that I was writing my way to my square of the quilt, taking
my slow place among the women I was only then learning to
know. Even Grandma herself. I'd never realized before how
entirely separate she was from me. I had only ever seen her
as my grandmother, and yet when I thought of the quilt, I

couldn't imagine what quote she might have considered, what symbol. A flag? A garden hoe? The sea? I'd lived with her most of my life, but I could never have sewn her square if she had asked.

But she knew how to sew Cecily's. With the quilt spread before me one afternoon, I noticed for the first time how similar the stitching was on Grandma's square and on Cecily's. The shape of the letter "A." The signature curl to the C. Grandma knew the two names after Morris, knew the way Cecily wanted to be remembered, and only Grandma would have stitched them on, pulled the patchwork that was Cecily into place.

Grandma could have left her out entirely, but one day, she had taken the time to include her. An imperfect remembrance.

That was the easy part to write. The part that was both anger and forgiveness, love and hate.

IN MID-FEBRUARY, THE snow slowed, and then stopped, and I cleared through it, headlights on. At the nursing home, the nurses had pasted little red hearts on every door, even 129. I paused at the nurse's station, staring at the string of hearts lining the hallway.

Kirsten put her hands on her hips. "What did you write this time?"

"Nothing incendiary," I said.

Kirsten looked skeptical, but I knew what was in the envelope. The part about Grandma. I wrote her as I saw her, as a woman, not as a relation. I wrote about her as if I were reporting, and she stepped off the page for me, became something I had never even glimpsed before. Whole.

Kirsten took a deep breath. She said, "You need a job."

"Will you tell her I'm here?" I wouldn't go see Grandma until I had a sense of what my reception would be.

Kirsten checked her watch. "Let me give Mortimer his pill."

I was sitting in the nursing home hallway when the light over 129 flickered, then again, on the board at the empty nurse's station. I hurried down the hall. Grandma lay in bed, eyes closed. I touched her shoulder, and she didn't open her eyes, she simply took my hand. That was all she wanted.

When she opened her eyes later, she stared at me for a while. But she held on.

"Who will apologize first?" I asked.

"How dare you quote the Bible to me." She sat up slowly. "I raised you to have opinions," she said, "but I did not raise you to disagree with me."

I laughed.

"I am apologizing first," she said.

My grandmother read her section while I was there. She tilted her lamp down over the pages, and when her eyes got tired, I read to her. We leaned into each other, shoulder to shoulder, out of habit. I described her first job at the five and dime; described how Cecily, whom she had so often defended, turned on her; described the salvaging of one lock of hair. I said that love had an amazing capacity to endure.

Grandma did not speak for a long time, and when she did, she said little, as though she had run out of words. She said, "You stuck to the facts."

I nodded.

Grandma looked at me. She picked up my hand, uncannily like hers. "You give me more credit than I deserve."

I remember a rush of feeling, that sudden relief and sadness, a sadness I had not expected and could not contain. I remember Grandpa, hand out, shaking, reaching for the pages. I remember Grandma opening her dresser drawer and pointing to the curl.

"Do you trust me to keep it?" she asked, and I nodded.

"I trust you, too," Grandma said. She stared at the clock. "What time is it?" she asked.

"Six o'clock."

"Time for current events," she said. I handed her her walker.

"You better write Cecily yourself," Grandma said. She spoke at the turn, when she would go right, to the rec room and the assembled rows of chairs, and I would go left, to the lobby, to the parking lot, and home.

"What?"

"I don't want to write anymore."

"I won't write this myself."

My grandmother rattled down the hall with her walker.

"Don't ever turn your back on me," I said. My voice carried, and Grandma turned back toward me, her face expressionless. Farther down the hall, I saw a nurse poke her head out of a bedroom, another take a tentative step our way, then pause.

My grandmother raised her hand, palm flat against the air as if she was pushing open a door. Then her hand twisted, moved in the air, like she was waving or tossing something off. The gesture was my benediction.

She said, "You tell them yourself. Tell them all. But do us justice, or I'll haunt you." Then she laughed. "I could do it, you know."

As I watched her go, I nodded, having no doubt that she would haunt me all my life.

SONS

WHEN I WAS eight, my father woke me in the middle of the night to watch a calf being born. I woke to the rolling, rich sound of his laughter, then boards creaking as he climbed the stairs. Before I could drift back to sleep on my warm, soft feather tick, my door opened. I smelled the cold air on him, a whiff of manure, and sat up in bed.

"Harry," he said, "get up."

In the kitchen, he handed me my first cup of coffee. The coffee tasted bitter, and I set the mug down, believing nothing could be worth all this trouble. But my father was alive that night, as if on fire, as if someone had set a light inside him. He glowed.

My father grabbed me by the hand, and we jogged across the yard. The night air was cold. Subzero temperatures slapped

me awake. Our boots crunched the snow as we ran. I will remember this always, this jog to the barn in the middle of the
night with only the light of the stars. I couldn't quite keep up
with my father, whose legs bore him forward in great strides.

Our three, one-story barns stretched long and low in front
of us. My father pushed open the door to the second, ushering
me inside. The barn was flooded with light, which made me
blink. I wanted to stop to catch my breath, but my father's
palms rested on my shoulders, propelled me forward to the
far end of the barn, where Dr. Vargas with his pointy beard
stood, a black bag opened at his feet and his arm stuck up to
the elbow in one of our cows' back end.

I started to leave.

"No, no, no," my father said, grabbing me by the shoulder
and pulling me back. "This is okay. This is life."

Dr. Vargas laughed, then lowered his head. His forehead
wrinkled. He spoke to my father. "This will be a difficult one,
James."

The cow moaned.

I looked up at my father, whose hands still rested on my
shoulders. "What's he doing?" I asked.

Then my father did something that focused my undivided
attention on that moaning cow. My father spoke to me in
Swedish.

He said, *"Titta här, Smulan."* Look.

My father called me Smulan affectionately. In Swedish, Smulan means crumb.

I THINK OF this now as I sit in a dimly lit hallway, listening to the nurses on the night shift tell each other about their Christmas plans. I can't see them well from where I sit. I see only the circular, mauve desk surrounding them, the pool of white light that bathes it. The pool of light reminds me of the barn, reminds me that the calf's birth is the only birth I've ever seen, reminds me that watching a calf being born is no preparation.

My father was wrong. That was not life.

One of the nurses laughs, and the sound of her laughter carries down the hall past me. I stand and rub my eyes. I wonder what time it is. I'm not wearing my watch. I'm wearing jeans and a sweatshirt, a down jacket and slippers. Megan's slippers, which are pink. I think of how she looked tonight as we raced to the car, biting her lip, holding her tummy, one wayward brown curl falling in her eyes; of the thin, tense smile she gave me as the nurses rolled her down the hall and away from me.

My father and mother are waiting for my second phone call. I imagine them now, sitting at the kitchen table. My mother has her hands wrapped around a coffee mug, and my father is leaning back on the two back legs of his chair, feet propped on the table, smoking his pipe. I imagine that my mother is watching the clock and shaking her head. And I imagine that my father is deferring to my mother's experience, letting her shake her head, letting her mutter, "This is not good."

When I called her from the lobby phone not too long ago, that was what she said: "This is not good."

We know we have a boy. We just didn't expect him this soon.

Farther away, in St. Paul, Megan's parents wait, trapped inside their house by a sudden December blizzard. I can't imagine them clearly. Maybe Mrs. Hall is making coffee. When in crisis, she usually does. Mr. Hall is probably clenching the keys to his Chevy Impala, waiting for the snow to stop. Most likely though, he has decided not to wait, just like my son. Instead, he is sliding down 94 East with Mrs. Hall, following the headlights to western Wisconsin and to the small hospital where I stand now, listening to nurses laugh.

My parents will not come.

I stand and stretch my legs, then lean against the wall. I don't understand the waiting. My mother's voice, soft and low, echoes in my head. "This is not good."

But waiting doesn't matter, as long as everything turns out all right. There is no price I would not pay.

THE CALF WAS breech, so Dr. Vargas had to turn it around. He stuck his arm inside the cow almost up to his shoulder, placed his free hand on her backside, and worked on turning that baby calf. The cow moaned, and when she did Dr. Vargas whispered to her. He whispered that she would be all right. He nodded to himself. Yes, she would be fine.

Then Dr. Vargas lifted his chin and grinned at my father. "Here it comes."

Dr. Vargas slowly pulled his arm out of the cow. His arm was smeared with blood, and the shirt sleeve he had pulled up to his elbow was stained. As his hand came out of the cow, his fingers were gripping two hooves.

I remember I stepped closer and watched as the skinny legs emerged, and then a nose, and finally, in a great rush, the whole heavy body wet with birth. Dr. Vargas caught the calf against his chest and laid it gently on the straw next to the cow. I stared at the shivering calf at my feet. Its eyes were open. It looked at me, and I stared back.

Dr. Vargas smiled at me, stretching his mouth so wide that his beard stretched as well and became even more pointed.

"Not bad for a night's work, eh, Harry?" he said.

I heard my father behind me. "He's never seen a calf being born before."

WE HAD THREE barns then. Later, we tore down the third because we had fewer cows, because the barn was too old. We expected to rebuild, but we didn't have the latest equipment, the size, or the clout to convince the bank to give us a loan. We were a family business. We relied on our reputation, but our reputation wouldn't pay the bills. The older I grew, the worse we did. We lost business. We scaled back. We got by.

I HAVE LOST track of time, and I search the pale yellow wall for a clock. A sketch of a barn and silo is on the hospital wall. I feel suddenly like I'm lost in a shopping mall, looking at a floor plan for the red triangle which will tell me where I am, orient me. But this picture doesn't orient me. This picture tells me where I am not.

My father and I don't speak any more. Whenever I call, my mother answers the phone. She apologizes for him. She asks if Megan and I are okay, listens to my yes, then quickly tells me that Mr. Hendrickson wants our cows. She still calls them our cows, as if I have a claim to them. I say nothing.

On rare occasions, she asks about my job. I lie. I don't tell her that I miss hearing the cows lowing. I don't explain how much I miss watching the sun rise behind the barns or eating family meals around our aged, wood table or drinking Dad's bad coffee, thick as sludge. Some things cannot last; some things last too long.

I am tempted to ask one of the nurses what time it is, but then I think, I don't really want to know.

MY GREAT-GRANDPA PATRIK left Sweden when he was 18. He came here, to Wisconsin, and married an American girl. He was not interested in talking about Sweden; he was not interested in lutefisk and lefsa and Aquavit. He insisted on speaking English. Patrik said this country was paradise.

Now our family can no longer speak Swedish. Our linguistic skills have deteriorated with each generation. We are reduced to tapping glasses together and saying *Skal*. We are left with only pieces of my great-grandfather's past, with only part of the truth, with only his surname, Kvist. What we have in common with Patrik is exactly what he intended.

Out here in this flat expanse of land, the wind gathers strength as it rolls across the prairie. Hits a man square in the face with cold and snow and sometimes ice. This is the same wind my ancestors endured; this is the wind that beat against their faces until their skin was red and raw and rugged. For years, we have worked the same land, and we are marked more by the wind than by our name. Today, our surname means nothing. We are no more Swedish than my friend Marty Feinstein. But we are farmers. We have the leathery faces, the chapped lips and hands, which are our scars.

Or, at least, I did have them. My skin is healing, now that I'm not blasted by wind or standing in a cold barn stamping my feet. Now I sit at a wooden desk. I swivel back and forth in my chair when I talk on the phone. I tell farmers about fertilizer. Sometimes I call home, just to hear them answer. They no longer answer as Kvist's Dairy.

I used to ask my father about Sweden, ask him to tell me stories. When I was young, he'd indulge me. He'd tell me about his father, August, and his Uncle Peter, whom great-grandpa Patrik in his old age sometimes called Peir. They each had a farm, not too far from one another, but as far apart as possible. My father told me what he could, but he couldn't name people in old family photographs. He couldn't remember who played the accordion, though he suspected it was Uncle Peir. He couldn't remember the names of Patrik's parents, or whether or not Patrik's father farmed.

Once when he was drunk, my father told me about Christmases at Uncle Peir's farm, all three households gathering to cut the tree, then decorate the boughs. They sang Christmas carols, Uncle Peir always leading, always off-key, with my grandmother accompanying on the piano.

But this is as detailed as my father got.

I have stared at the pictures of these men, of August with his round glasses and curled mustache; of Uncle Peir with his sizable belly; of great-grandpa Patrik, who is squinting. I want to ask Patrik why he left us with nothing but photographs. Photographs and land in paradise.

I think, "You had too much confidence in this country, Great-Grandpa Patrik." The night my father told me about the family Christmases at Uncle Peir's, he slipped. Too much Aquavit. He leaned over the armrest of his chair, motioned me close with his hand. His breath was hot and wet against my cheek when he spoke:

"My father told me that he thought Grandpa Patrik left Vimmerby because he killed a man."

Then he pushed me away, shook his head, said nothing for the rest of the evening. He fell asleep in his armchair, woke himself snoring, and lumbered off to bed. Sleep well, he muttered.

I don't know if my father remembers his slip.

I'll never know what he knows or doesn't know.

AT THE OPPOSITE end of the hall, past the nurses' station, there are vending machines. I walk the length of the hall, Megan's slippers slapping on the tile. When I pass the nurses they lower their voices. I keep my head down. I don't want to speak to them. I don't want their sympathetic smiles.

THE CALF THAT was born became my training bull. My father lectured me on its development. As the calf grew, he explained to me what weight he needed it to be. This was not a bull my father planned to keep; he made this clear immediately. He said, "Don't name the calf, Harry." The bull was good stock, but we didn't need another, and we could get a good price for him. And

I didn't cry when the bull was carted off with others we didn't plan to keep. My father said, this is the life of a farmer, and I understood. I have always understood.

In early October, I walked downstairs from Megan's and my upstairs bedroom, from the converted attic that was our apartment within the house, and told my father I was going to stop farming. We had had the first snow then, and the morning air was rejuvenating or maybe without the wind, the cold just didn't bother me.

I said, "Dad, let's go for a walk."

But we didn't. I got as far as the back steps and sat down. I couldn't move. The sun was rising, and suddenly I didn't want to walk. I didn't want to say anything. I wanted to stay.

Dad met me on the steps with a freshly brewed cup of coffee.

He said, "This house is too old and too small."

He was smoking a cigarette, rubbing his trim white beard. He wore his black rubber boots.

"Maybe we can fix up the house ourselves this spring. I said, "Dad..."

He shook his head and took a sip of his coffee. "Don't worry about the money. We'll manage."

"Dad..."

Maybe the tone of my voice betrayed me, because his eyes immediately met mine. He stared at me, and I looked away.

Away from the barns, away from the Swedish flag snapping against the flagpole beside the house, away from my father. Away from the land I had planned never to leave.

And then, as the sky settled into the washed-out gray of a winter sky, Dad asked: "What will you do?"

"I've lined up a job with Hansen's Fertilizer in Eau Claire."

"I see. You've been thinking about this for a while, then."

I nodded.

"You should have told me earlier." Then my father was silent. Suddenly he said: "I can't do this alone."

We have not spoken since.

THESE ARE THE things my son will not know: the first dark morning of winter when stars freckle the sky as we head out to do chores; the chorus of cows lowing as they come back into the barn from pasture; the taste of milk fresh from the cow.

This is what kills me, deep down. Not that my childhood is slipping away, or my way of life. Not that the last tangible evidence of my past is up for sale. What kills me is that my son will never know what the seasons smell like on a farm. My son will not know in his bones how a farm works. My son will not understand me.

We are two families now, the family that farmed, and the family that will not.

THE EVENING MEGAN and I left the farm, just as we were about to climb into my truck, my father pulled me aside. He said nothing, he simply tugged at my jacket sleeve. I walked with him down the driveway, waiting for him to speak. We walked in silence past the house, past the flagpole, down the driveway, to the first barn. He pulled open the door, and we walked by each cow. As we passed they turned their heads, glanced at us, then looked away. We walked out the door at the other end, then into the second barn, past the empty stalls, over the scrubbed floor. He stopped finally at the far end of the barn, and I understood what he could not say.

MY FATHER WILL wait up until the phone rings. He won't go to bed. And perhaps tonight when I call, he'll get on the phone. Perhaps tonight we'll speak, if only of the baby.

I see the doctor. He's standing at the nurses' station, dressed in his blue paper gown, discussing something with the nurses. He turns in my direction, and I stand. And suddenly I'm walking as I imagine Mr. Hall is driving, as perhaps my father is driving, coming from the other direction, west to his grandchild, west to his son.

"Mr. Kvist, you have a son. He weighs three pounds. Amazingly, no defects." The doctor is smiling at me. I can't remember his name.

"Will he live?" My voice sounds hoarse.

The doctor pushes his glasses up on his nose. "I can't say he'll survive, but I have high hopes."

I can live with high hopes. I notice there is blood on his blue paper gown, and I stare at him, waiting.

Finally I say, "How's my wife?"

"She's fine," he says.

"I want to see them."

I walk with him down the hall, past the nurses' station, down another hall, and into a room. Megan is asleep, her head to one side. She is pale and drawn. I kiss her forehead, but she doesn't open her eyes.

The doctor stands on the other side of her bed.

"She's fine," he repeats.

I hold her hand. I wipe her forehead though it is dry and cool. I listen to her breathe.

"Would you like to meet your son?"

I glance up at the doctor, at his round, flushed face, at his broad smile, at the wire glasses he wears.

The doctor calls for a nurse to guide me. She leads me to an elevator, and we ride up two floors. We walk through double doors, past another nurses' station, past an old man whom someone has left sitting in the hallway in a wheelchair.

We stop in front of a large glass window that looks into a room full of babies, terrifyingly small babies. They have tubes sticking in their nostrils, tubes taped with white tape to their arms. I search the bassinets. I search among the faces of the babies for one who looks windblown.

I see my son. I know him instantly.

He is the one who is screaming.

"A kid like that has to live," I tell the nurse, and I mean this as an order.

I have a son now, a three-pound son. A three-pound son with no name. But unlike the product of the only birth I've seen, this one will be named. This one I will keep.

The nurse stands beside me for a moment, then mutters something I can't hear and leaves. I place my forehead against the glass and watch my son. I watch another nurse go over to him, put her hands in little gloves which are made to fit inside his incubator, adjust a tube which is in his arm, check the tube in his nose. He is too little for tubes. The tubes must be bigger than his veins.

I speak to him through the glass. I whisper: *"Titta här, Smulan."*

My son stops screaming. I flatter myself that somehow he knows I am here.

I don't know what to say to my son, so I begin to recite my memories. I begin by telling him about his grandfather and about the night his mother and I left the farm, left the house that had been my home for thirty years, and drove to Eau Claire. I tell him about the walk my father and I took, about the smell of the cows and the chill in the air that whispered of snow. I tell him that my father and I did not hug good-bye, that we stood facing each other, staring at each other, until he turned and walked back into the house.

I tell Smulan that as I watched my father walk away, I knew how I would remember my father: half eaten by dusk, halfway back to the house, half with me and half not. And I promise Smulan that I'll ask for my father when I call home tonight; that when we are done speaking of him, I will ask my father what he really knows about great-grandpa Patrik.

GEOGRAPHIES OF THE HEART

THE NIGHT OUR grandfather died was a night without stars, the snow falling in endless repeat, first veiling the moon, the constellations, then the sharp edges of buildings – our whole world. Toward the end, when my grandfather seemed only to be lingering of his own will, I stood outside the main entrance of the hospital, looking for headlights; stunned by the deep and unsettling quiet of St. Paul under snow and then by the long keening wail of a siren inching toward Emergency, the neon lights there obscured by snow and ice and hope.

It was a night of mourning, and the mourning had come early. Grandpa had slipped beyond us at dusk, the rattle of his breathing slowly losing energy and force, the night lengthening and darkening with each diminished breath. Upstairs, my family huddled in his cramped room or took turns pacing the hall outside, each footstep measured like a heartbeat and almost as constant. We leaned against one another, against the pressure of what was coming as slowly and stealthily as that snow, wild in the wind outside yet silent. We leaned past dusk into nighttime, and as the night went on, we listened to his struggling breaths and held our own. In the end he gasped.

Before he died, I took the elevator down to the lobby and phoned my sister. It was the third time that day I'd tried to reach her. She wasn't home, as usual. Still, I listened for her answer, and I watched the main entrance, hoping to see her slide through the doors, riding in on the edge of this latest snowstorm in a blossom of white, a brief rush of cold. It was late then, and while she could have gotten to the hospital earlier, I doubted she would make it now, and I wondered where she was. She had known how fast Grandpa was deteriorating. She had known, just as I had, to be ready for the phone to ring. And so I called, one last time.

This was during the first week of November. I had not talked to Glennie in weeks. For the length of the fall, she had remained noticeably absent, despite calls for company, for help with the baby. Despite our obvious, looming loss. I was twenty-four then, and she was twenty-one. She was finish-ing her second to last semester at the U, and she had recently begun calling at odd hours, when I wasn't home, and leaving messages like telegrams. *Am fine. Talk soon. Kiss Amelia. Hi to Al.* She shrank into a line, all bone and tumbling gold hair, and devoted herself with religious intensity to school.

At the start of the semester she had spent her free evenings drafting lengthy essays for medical school applications. In her brief appearances, over coffee down by the university, at our house for dinner, she always wore the same Gopher sweatshirt and a pair of running tights. She chewed her nails. She looked paler than I thought was possible, the rich yellow of her hair making her skin look alabaster, the fineness of her bones growing more prominent. I had tried to talk to her, me leaking with milk that stained my blouses, me with the warmth and curves Amelia had given me, but Glennie's answers were perfunctory, her gaze drifting elsewhere. She was waiting, she said, to hear; and so it seemed she could not listen. I thought of all this that night at the hospital, staring out from the phone cubby into the white of the storm. But I thought she would come, in one last show of love. In the end.

I waited a long time with that phone receiver in my hand, listening to the flat, buzzing ring. The phone rang so long that the operator finally cut in and asked if I was all right. Her voice had startled me. I thought she was Glennie. I said, "It's Sarah. You better come now."

When I hung up the phone and walked outside into that silent new world, searching for sight of her car, I reminded myself that she would have phoned if she'd been stranded.

We would know. The quiet, interrupted in fits and starts by a siren, then a howl of wind, was broken finally by the ambulance itself, pressing against the wind; against the onslaught of snow. And then again, that deep quiet filled the night. I waited until the cold sent me back inside. And when I turned back to the elevators alone, I turned like others in my family had turned before me, some like milk, others like fall leaves, a little more sour, or ready to crumble at the touch. I turned and something twisted in me when I did.

THAT WINTER, THERE were constant reminders of Grandpa's passing with the holidays to background his absence, with Glennie's strange new behavior to accentuate all the change. When I was growing up, we had all lived in one house, the generations piled in layers, like the number of floors: three. Every time I went over to Mom and Dad's, the downstairs where Grandpa had lived was silent and gaping, and I realized again how much he'd marked my growing up, how I'd lived less by a clock than by his rituals: his alarm clock sounding into the early morning and waking me where I slept upstairs, or the chinking sound of the beer cap falling onto the kitchen counter at five o'clock, when he pulled a chair onto the front porch and watched cars drive by. I'd often joined him, and he would tell me what I was seeing: a house finch, cumulus clouds, an '84 Ford. I had grown up fingering the yellowed newspapers that had announced D-Day and Kennedy's assassination. I had watched the ritual picking of the cucumber yield and their slow progression into sweet pickles, Grandma patiently stirring, Grandpa quick to swear if he sliced a finger, which he'd wag at me. I understood references to the point system and knew old Navy jokes that no small child should know. I learned when to fold in a poker game. Every room held a slim memory, like a sleeve.

DURING GRANDPA'S LAST few weeks I kept an old list in my wallet of what medicines he took and for what ailments, out of habit and just in case. I kept a separate old list of doctors' names and beeper numbers. And toward the end, when the world reeled in that endless snow, I kept vigil, shooting straight up in bed each late night the phone rang, or not even sleeping at all but staring out the window, watching the next storm ride in.

I made two emergency trips to the hospital that winter, once in the early afternoon, when Mom had taken a break and gone home, and once on Halloween, at dawn, when my car was the only one that started, coughing and spitting into the morning with all the reluctance I felt. The exhaust rose behind the car like a premonition.

His doctor had told us that Grandpa's systems would slow and then stop one by one, as if someone were systematically going through a house and shutting off all the lights. I still haven't gotten over that image. And that last cold October morning, with my Honda sputtering in the cold, with Amelia snug in her car seat and smiling against what seemed to me a gray and dismal day, I wondered what was stopping now for Grandpa, what system had finally come to rest.

At the hospital I'd handed over the soft, worn lists and watched as a nurse unfolded them and scanned the names and numbers. Yes, she told me, we have this information. I let my thoughts drift to Glennie, who had left another breathy message on my machine the night before. Her voice had sounded tentative. *Really busy. Can't talk. Call me.* I had instead stumbled to bed, guilty for not calling but swept with a fatigue deeper and more rooted than any I'd ever known. Now there I was in the hospital, wondering where she was and what the hell was wrong. I wondered if she was okay. But of course she wasn't, and I knew it.

The nurse called Dr. Hines, her voice low; and when she knew her answers, and I knew Grandpa would be all right, when I had sat with him for a minute and fixed his hair and covered his feet with a blanket; after I had called my mother and she had calmed down; after this I lifted my cooing and beautiful daughter higher on my hip and marched us both over to the row of pay phones to call the sister who was narrowing. Herself, her heart. And mine.

I left Glennie a message. About fatigue and Grandpa and the baby. My voice was sharp. I demanded to know what the hell was wrong. I was holding Amelia in the crook of one arm, and she crowed into the receiver, leaving an aria for her aunt, who barely seemed to have words left, or the energy to speak them. We MacMillan women, thin-skinned from an overabundance of snow and sadness, let words lodge like icicles inside us. We froze.

What the hell, I had said into the receiver.

Glennie later told me she'd needed a break that winter, but a break from what I've never fully known. Never once did she make it to the hospital before Grandpa died. She did not help sort through his things. She called Mom and Dad, leaving messages in the same telegraphed language, which heaped one worry upon another, and she arrived at the funeral looking disheveled and as bitten as her nails. And this is where it begins, rising like a blister over the same worn spot. One might imagine we are too old for old grievances, that we have moved beyond. But how do you move past an absence like hers without taking notice?

Distance doesn't always make the heart grow fonder. Sometimes, I've learned, it makes the heart grow harder. But I called. Finally. It had been years since Glennie and I had really talked. Our conversations usually circled the controversial and relied on the secure, though even then I had a tendency for the quick jab, the sarcastic remark. She'd come by and have dinner, maybe linger over a drink at some brief happy hour, but I didn't know the details of her days or what she thought about the M.D. now that she had it, after all those years of fight. I didn't know her any more, or she me; and so I took a look at my calendar one morning, saw my thirtieth birthday approaching, and decided to give myself a gift. I'd take her on a mini-vacation. Pull her out of her hospital, away from her milieu and away from mine, and on neutral territory we'd try to connect again, not with who we were or what we'd shared in the past, but with who we had become.

I'd laugh if I felt like laughing: she was still impossible to reach. I had to leave a message. So I did, a staccato, stammering message that made me feel a sliver of recognition, like a shiver. I said: *It's me. Your sister. Please call.*

I HADN'T PLANNED anything extravagant. A bed and breakfast, a three-day weekend, maybe a little more wine than usual. I planned only for us to get away, as if that effort alone overtaxed my imagination.

I arrived at her hospital late in the afternoon. It was hot for April, steaming even, and I kept the station wagon running and aimed every vent in my direction, let the tepid air bother loose a strand of hair. A fistful of daffodils bloomed at the base of the flagpole, and every once in a while the flag lifted with the breeze and a ripple passed over the clutch of blooms. I let my head fall back against the seat. I closed my eyes.

Her hospital, which is what I have always called it for no clear reason, was in St Paul; her apartment nearby, within a stone's throw, as my grandfather might have said. The drive from our house was short, but we didn't make the route often, Al, Amelia and I. We dropped by on holidays. Remembered her birthday. We had perfected--I had required that we per-fect--the brief, cheery visit. The fifteen-minute family.

The station wagon was a relic from the 1970s that Al had magically, and with great love, revived over the course of spring semester. Early on Saturday mornings, when his only company was an occasional house finch or the low rush of a passing car, or occasionally a curious Amelia drawn by the clanking and crashing and frequent string of curses, Al backed the wagon out of the garage and tinkered, got his mind away from papers and books and students, from the heavy questions which defined his profession.

Al had never looked like a religion professor, rounded as he was, and with his white-blond hair. He looked like an ath-letic coach, a man who could cheer his team on to great feats. And he did. Each semester, he cheered on the students who refused to work or read, who called his assignments too hard because, in effect, they did not want to think. He had graded the first round of papers that spring with a sagging spirit of optimism. Then, halfway through the semester, with a stack of miserable midterms dominating the dining-room table, he found the car. I think it came from a junkyard, but it may have come from Larch, an aged family friend who still runs a bar downtown and seems to accumulate all sorts of strays. Suddenly the car appeared in the driveway, rusted, with two flat rear tires and a caved-in driver's side panel. And Al beamed. He thought it was wonderful.

The station wagon had fake paneling on the sides and a rich blue accent and when I drove it, the car hummed like it was happy to be back on the road. *I* was happy to be back on the road, packed for a vacation.

"There ought to be room," I had said to Al that morning, "for Glennie and I to grow apart and come back together again. There ought to be a little room for fluctuations."

But I was really saying that I hoped there was. She may be the surgeon, and I the mother, but we came from the same places, the same hopes. We had to understand a little of one another, enough at least to share new ground. We were sisters, after all.

And that's what I kept thinking as she tumbled through the hospital doors, wriggling out of her white coat as she walked, each footstep efficient and clipped. She looked like a race walker as she came toward me, elbows jutting into the air. She climbed in, loosening the bun that held her hair and like her it tumbled, hair that I've always loved.

"We're off!" she said, raising her hands and laughing, her laugh flickering, light, resonating throughout the car.

For a moment, I stared at her, uncertain, but then I nodded.

Yes, we were off.

This was it.

Finally, despite all distractions, despite even ourselves, we were going.

I REMEMBER THE oddest things about the winter Grandpa died. I remember in detail how the sun looked coming into the kitchen early one morning, falling in a lazy, generous beam, and how quiet the kitchen was. Al was asleep, Amelia was asleep, and I sat alone with a cup of peppermint tea, relishing the solitude. But a great deal else is only an impression. The hospital is a blur of white, as are the roads I traveled to and from; even Amelia learning to roll and chirping her first word (car) are memories crushed like flowers against the pages of a long, dense book, one that rivals for attention, one that demands.

But I remember Glennie.

Downstairs, curled on our sagging leather couch, exhausted from the semester, she slept through most of Christmas and we did not wake her. Al played pinball softly on Grandpa's old machine, but even when the bells and whistles clanked and sang, even when he hooted in victory, Glennie slept on, like a bear in hibernation, like the princess poisoned.

I watched her sleeping once. I placed my hand in front of her face until her breath moved softly against my skin, and I stayed to make sure her breathing remained even. Maybe this is the root of all trouble in my family, or in me: fear. I checked to make sure Glennie was still alive, drove the silent winter roads to Grandpa consumed by dread; she stayed away, then after the new year stood at the mailbox in the dead of winter, half-covered in an ill-fitting down jacket, waiting for her grades. All As, but not a glimmer of relief in her eye, just a look harder and more determined, as if she were doing calculations in her head. And I believe that she was. She was figuring her chances, the percentages, her acceptance rate. She hit it on the head, too. So dispassionate, so objective. She looked at herself like a pool of admissions counselors would and knew what to expect.

But what had she lost that winter to do it? Always, like a rumor, something insidious and whispery inside my heart: what had she let go of to become so cool?

IN THE CAR, Glennie rolls down her window and lets her head fall back against the seat.

"God," she says. "What a day. I kept thinking that all I had to do was to get through it, and then I'd be on the road."

"Me, too."

Glennie looks at me. "This will be fun," she says, and I am grateful for her effort, her small offering.

"Yes," I say, pressing my foot on the gas.

Somewhere outside of Minneapolis we break down. I should have known to take the Honda, I guess, but the large floating-boat feel of the station wagon appealed. The space appealed. And Al was so proud of it.

It is sweltering and dry on the highway, and gusts of warm air balloon toward us, gently rocking the car. My shirt is cool against my back, and I imagine what I look like: sweat rings darkening the underarms of my white blouse, my hair pulled back but falling in wisps, and wetly, around my face; the lines around my eyes and mouth, the tired look to my gaze. The day is slipping away, near dusk, and neither of us know a damn thing about cars.

It doesn't take long to find a gas station, since we'd just passed a ramp heading into a small town. The attendant, an older man with gray hair and a deeply lined face, agrees to give us a lift back in his tow truck, where he says he'll hazard a guess. He drives us back onto the highway, back into the dry, slow wind, and toward the station wagon, which suddenly looks not much different to me than when I'd first seen it. I think of Al's careful attention, as careful as his commentary on papers, as thoughtful and precise, and I don't want it to fail, I don't want him to know.

"It's nothing," the old man says, and his voice is a whisper, dry like the wind, and as hot against my face.

He tows us back to his shop, and we sit thigh to thigh in the front seat, arm to arm, bumping down the ramp and into town. He smells of oil and dust, and Glennie smells of soap, something sharp that reminds me of spring. I know I'll remember that distinctly, that fresh smell off her in the heat.

Glennie and I walk through the highway underpass while the man works, shirtless, his back the sandy brown of a construction worker's and as smooth and muscular as a young man's. We steer ourselves past graffiti, around pop cans and stray plastic bags, past cigarette butts and random, sad purple flowers and walk the cracked sidewalk into downtown Belton, a pocket of shops nestled up against the highway.

Our choices are a steak house and fast food. We choose the steak house. We are our father's daughters, after all, raised on summer cookouts and the juicy first bite of steak; raised on the smell of it cooking. Inside, we slide our trays along the grooved countertop, craning our necks to see the menu. The restaurant is empty, save for the young chef finishing the last of his cigarette and a girl who piles droopy lettuce into a container for the salad bar. We choose a table in the center, under an air vent.

Glennie is hungry, but I've never known her to be less.

Hunger is in her. She is starving or famished but always thin, always a reed.

"Dad used to cook the best steaks," she says.

I glance at her. On the tip of my tongue are the familiar old words, the bad habit: *he still does*, but I check myself and perhaps she senses this because she looks at me while she swallows, and there we are, face to face with it, the same old tension.

I lift my coffee cup and take a long, slow, easy sip, letting the liquid fill me with something close to strength and security.

"Have you been over to Mom and Dad's lately?" she asks.

"I was there last night."

"How are things?"

"Things are fine. Things are good."

And it's true, or true enough. She ought to know that Mom complained of stiffness in her hands, of stiffness settling in her everywhere, as though she is filling with cement, but I tell Glennie things are fine and hope it spares the two of us something.

Glennie watches me. I nod, suddenly hesitant to give voice to my lie again. I hold my coffee cup in front of my face, look out the window at the highway, at the brightness of the day slowly receding.

"Mom's enjoying her garden," I say.

"It won't always be."

"What?"

"It won't always be fine," Glennie says.

I look at her over the rim of my coffee cup. I hadn't expected this, and I stare at her for a moment, then set down my cup. We have decisions coming. We have more farewells. But those were far off, and what seems more relevant to me is that we do not have each other.

"That isn't what we need to talk about," I say suddenly. "That's not what this weekend is about."

Glennie says, "Isn't it?"

ON THAT COLD night, when Minnesota blessed us with temperatures warm enough for snow and we gathered without Glennie to say goodbye to my grandfather, I let go of a tradition, of what I understood a family to be. The snow came down and piled itself softly as though to cushion the blows.

The hospital had a machine that cleared Grandpa's lungs, but he had waved it away the last time he'd had strength, and now we were down to it, as he might have said.

"We're all here," Dad had told him, squeezing his hand. "All here."

Al leaned out the door and asked for a nurse, and Nancy came in, her footsteps hushed against our breathing, her movements swift. Nancy, who had over the weeks taken a place among us. She gave him a painkiller, or maybe that's what I'd like to think, the memory of his breathing, of the fluid in his lungs, too much to bear without the slim memory of relief, true or not.

I don't remember Nancy leaving, only that when we filtered into the hall late that night she was there, arms spread outward, as if she could hold us all. Only that we listened to the rattle of his breathing, whispering him onward, whispering our love, until all we heard was ourselves.

I didn't ask Glennie why she never came to the hospital that night, nor did she volunteer, and I said only one thing to her when she finally did appear the next morning, rushing into the hospital restaurant. Dad and Al had left to call Larch, who even at his age, and in that snow, was already waiting in the lobby, waiting while they called him at home. Mom had gone to the ladies' room, and there were Glennie and I seated at a small table, staring at each other. She asked if he'd gone peacefully, and I wanted to break her in half. I was grieving, and afraid: of her, whom I no longer knew; of her pencil-thin wrists; of how supremely angry I was.

I looked at her and said, "Don't."

Al said maybe she couldn't handle what touched her family, but I've never agreed. How much would it have required of her to appear, even briefly? At any ceremony, at any ritual, there were always six of us, then seven and eight with Al and Amelia, and I could not believe, am slow to forgive, that my grandfather died without the full measure of support he was due; that one small voice did not join our chorus on the only day it mattered.

"What if she just isn't as strong as you?" Al asks.

The question passes into each new year despite my efforts to forgive, despite my best intentions. I know what he's wondering. Does she sometimes question me, too? But I question only Glennie. Not her competence. Not her brains. But her compassion, which I believe is essential to love.

This year, though, as the subject made its way to the surface once again, Al asked a different question. It was a Sunday. I'd dropped Amelia off at a friend's house and returned home with an armload of groceries and some grievance. A bad driver ahead of me, a surly grocery clerk. I don't remember, only that the irritation arose and transformed itself and grew and suddenly I was back in that hospital again, and Glennie was not.

"For God's sake," Al finally said, quietly, as he peered into the engine of his rusted renovation. "Sarah, what the hell is this really about?"

He turned to me, away from the car, accepted in silence the pop I had brought out to him.

"Family," I replied. "Values and commitment and family and love. It's about how we were raised. It's about a way of life. It's about her not being there. For any of us. And certainly not for me."

And there it was, in all its bald and ugly and broken self: *I* had needed her that night. *I* was tired of holding up, holding together, holding hands. I needed her, and she was not there, and she did not come to us, like we had hoped. She fled somewhere else, to someone else for comfort, and left me waiting, standing at the phone bank in the hospital lobby, alone.

I blinked at Al, who turned back to the car, his gaze out to the road.

"You're letting bitterness eat you alive," he said.

The cool air in the restaurant lowers a degree or two, and the background music abruptly switches to classical halfway through a whining and overdone love song.

I pause. "How are things with you?"

Glennie shrugs. "The same," she says. "People come to the hospital, and I try to help them, and sometimes I succeed."

I don't want to ask about failure. I can imagine what her feelings are. But I do want to know how she defines loss. At one time she'd confided, then at least gave the semblance of it, passing on news of boyfriends and school fears and snippets of dreams. But sitting there across from her, the two of us alone for the first time in years, I know she squirrels most of her life away; that we have broken apart, like continents, leaving a gaping ocean between us. She would not tell me what loss was, and I would not ask.

"Amelia shot up three inches this year," I say.

Glennie smiles. "She's going to be a tall one. One day you'll be looking in her eyes."

I laugh, but the laugh is short and high. I think, *someday we all have to look each other in the eye*, and I say what I've wanted to say for years.

"I've always been angry that you were never there." My voice sounds soft and even, but Glennie looks away, shakes her head.

"How much would it have taken out of you to be there for just a minute?" I ask, the question pressing forward with the weight of years.

"People aren't always perfect." She sounds worn at the edges, her answer running over my question.

"Were you eating at all?"

Glennie shoots me a glance, and her face, her jaw, seem rigid. The question goes unanswered.

"Where were you?"

She's staring out the window at the thin line of cars snaking along the highway, slowly for some odd reason, as if dusk is treacherous. And maybe it is. Dusk brought us to this place, where I no longer count on her, or she on me; where our roots fill different pots, and we reach for different light.

"He didn't know I wasn't there," she says, "so why do you care so much?"

I can't answer. Something inside me has suddenly ripped

open.

Glennie pulls her gaze away from the road and back to me. "Just because I wasn't there doesn't mean I wasn't grieving. I was."

Forget the peaceful landscape, forget the quiet bed and breakfast where we could drink wine to take the edge off. It is now, over steaks and coffee. It's here. I'm suddenly too tired to get angry. "Why couldn't you come, just for a little? Why couldn't you just say goodbye?"

I wait. I'm not good at waiting.

"I didn't want to be there," she says finally, leaning forward, her face close to mine. I smell the steak sauce on her breath, watch the lines shaping around her mouth, lines that I know are not laugh lines. I never look away.

"I'll never want to be there. For anyone."

"Then why are you even bringing up the subject of Mom and Dad?"

Glennie takes a deep breath, one that she seems to have been gathering for years. "I don't want to see the people I care about … I don't want to remember them that way."

"It's not about you." My voice sounds sharp and tight, and I blush instantly because it is all about her and me and only ever has been. I suddenly can't believe who we've become.

And then she says, "I was there. In my apartment."

She's looking straight at me. It takes a minute for the reference to sink in, and then it does.

"I'm sorry," I tell her. And I am. For both of us. For the ways we allow fear to preside. But she let me down, let us all down. She abandoned something I loved, and that makes me even sorrier.

Glennie squints her eyes. "Do you think you're the better person?"

I look at her, whose hands save lives, the thin fingers delicately putting back into place what has ripped away or broken down; whose precision is notorious.

"I think you should have been there," I tell her. "But mostly I think we're both selfish as hell and that Grandpa wouldn't like either one of us."

We sit quietly for a while and the restaurant fills in, and we are an island in the middle, sinking in spongy seats, seated at a hard plastic table, remembering.

I want to ask about hunger, about how she starved herself down to a nub in college, how she made it through medical school at all. I want to tell her that I have never been prouder of her than the day the provost slipped the mantle over her gown and pronounced her name, enunciated each syllable: Dr. Carys Glenn MacMillan. We rose in our seats in one loud roar, all of us, even Larch. I want to breathe into our afternoon something like a prayer for her, something like a hymn for me.

"I'll need you there," I say, my voice trailing off.

And then, as the truth drifts out into the hot and steaming day, our pick-up time for the car already past, my sister says, "Do you ever forgive?"

I look up at her sharply, ready to answer until I see her expression, the way her eyes search mine, as though I'm unknown to her; until I realize that she has told me what loss is. I don't like her very much, even though I love her, and I wonder what size I've made her feel over the years, how much a person like me can wear another down, or send a scar straight into the marrow, to stay. I wonder how much she likes me.

We're from the same place, but we have different geographies of the heart.

I stare at her narrow frame with that hair like a prize and think: she consumed herself that winter, allowed herself to be consumed. She left us on the edge of her world, left my grandfather outside it, left simply and for good a part of her heart in the frozen landscape of that endless, relentless winter.

But so did I.

The restaurant is filling in, a family tucking into salads, not a word spoken, their attention focused on their bowls. An old man sits alone, his eyes rheumy and faraway, like Glennie's now, again. Like everything, suddenly. Faraway and hard to see.

I take a deep breath. "I'm going to go. I am going to go to this bed and breakfast."

Nothing in her expression changes, and so I force myself.

Rise above. God, I'm sick of her. Mostly, though, I'm sick of myself.

"Are you coming?" I ask.

I wait. She turns toward me again and before I can let her say no, before I can bear up under the force of whatever her expression reveals, I take my chance. I know it is our last. I say, "Come."

We walk out into the hot day in step but grimly so. The day is dim, and the glow is almost gone, one last streak of light in the horizon. We walk under the highway, past the garbage and the empty coke cans and the scrawled messages of violence and love, and I know I will never forget the heat, though the day has cooled; I will never forget walking with her back to the small gas station, with its one pump and that old man behind the counter, who let us go with only a wave.

We climb into the car and thread our way back through the side streets to the ramp, and we shoot off, our red taillights disappearing into the open dark of the road. We don't sing any old songs we know; don't tell each other stories; don't relive what past there is to share. We go forward against some great falling crush. The ride is long, and we ride in a kind of relief, glad for the movement because movement feels like hope, driving toward the reconciliation beyond us, but there, like a beacon, or a constellation.

MOTHERLY

OUTSIDE, CHILDREN SKATE on a homemade ice rink. Their multi-colored coats weave an odd kind of tapestry in the yellow winter light. They skate on what is left of a field, a place where in the summer I can still spot the prairie grass and mustard flowers. The houses butting up against the rink are gray, and tan, then gray again; they repeat, like a melody, the three designs that the Oldsheiger Construction Company uses.

I sit in what was once my mother's home, looking out the window at the skaters and their houses. This house is no repeat. My father and my uncles built it over the course of two years, rushing to finish before I was born in winter 1949. They drank whiskey the night they finished, drank whiskey and tore up and down the fields in my Dad's tractor, waving their arms and cracking jokes and trying to make the tractor go fast. I know because my mother told me once when reminiscing.

The house is warm, and I have the radio on to keep me company. A trumpet concerto plays softly, sounding triumphant and robust, and yet the house feels full of quiet, unnaturally quiet, as if the phone ought to be ringing, or the doorbell, or an alarm.

Yesterday Jenny turned to walk into her college orientation without saying good-bye; then, as though I was an afterthought, she waved. She was in a crowd of girls from her dormitory, all new to that out-of-state school, and I watched them walk into the red brick building clumped together. Before the crowd slipped through the door, a hand shot up and waved.

I am sure that hand was hers.

1972. THE COLD came early in the season, before the burnt orange colors of October reached their prime, before the leaves turned and dropped and we could rake them into piles for Jenny to jump into. The fields had yellowed in the first days of the month, like the pages of an old newspaper, and wiped away what green the summer had left us; and we prepared for fall, pulling windbreakers out of the cedar chest and hanging Indian corn on the front doors. Jenny was in Kindergarten then.

When the first blast of chill air blew down in a great arc from the north, we were caught off guard. The cold killed the pumpkin crop, and up and down the road the crooked smiles on each doorstep began to look sunken and toothless, like old people. And then the snow came, falling in a whisper so that at first, no one noticed.

The snow started falling when the kids lined up on the corner for the school bus, and the snow fell long after the bus brought them back home. In mid-afternoon the bus appeared out of the white haze in flashes of yellow, the rumble of its engine muted by the steady, heavy snow. I walked toward the blurs of color which I knew were children, searching. I took children by the shoulders, by the elbows, and turned them round until I could see their faces. When Jenny looked up at me, lashes already laced with snowflakes, I could not speak. I reached for her hand and leaned in close. Older children quickly peeled away in packs, and we stood in the soundless snow and watched them disappear.

I HAVE LIVED in this Minnesota town most of my life, and I have never known a day as bitter as that day in October with Jenny. Even the storm which raged through town when I was ten was less threatening than the quiet, constant, thick accumulation of snow that October of 1972.

The blizzard which tore through town when I was ten was full of wind and whirling snow and made of a cold raw enough to kill a man. I dressed to go outside, and my little brother, Ray, followed. We didn't think anything of sneaking

out the back door for a minute or two. We tried to see Carter's bulky red barn across the long fields or the lights in the
windows of his house, but coming at us, right in our face, was
what seemed like currents of snow, and at first, we laughed.

The wind pushed us forward, and we gripped each other's
hands. We walked slowly, aiming for our barn or Carter's or
the fence between the two, for anything, but the cold got to us.
The wind bit at us through our coats and wool sweaters and
jeans, and the snow wet our faces, and then the wetness froze.
When we tried to talk, the wind stole our voices and threw
them up into the storm. The cold bore into my bones, and my
bones turned brittle, like icicles. When Raymond saw lights, I
was too tired to walk to them, and he herded me home.

Mom was too angry at us to yell. She handed us each a
warm towel and a cup of hot chocolate and made us sit in
front of the fire. When she finally spoke, she said, "That was
stupid, Carol." I should have tape recorded that, to save my
mother from having to repeat herself down through the years.

My mother had looked to my father, eyebrows raised,
but he said nothing. But the next morning before we went to
school, he took us out into the backyard. He showed us little
indentations in the snow, what was left of our footprints.

We had been walking in circles.

"You could have been out here 'til you froze, just trying
to find the back door," Dad had said. He was smoking a cig-

arette. He smoked so much then that he seemed to have six fingers on one hand. "Why'd you go outside anyway?"

Neither of us could answer. Ray hit me in the arm, but I stared at the footprints and shook my head.

"Winter's no thing to play around with," Dad said. "You think winter is all snowmen and hot chocolate and ice skating and Christmas at the end. Well," he said. "Well."

The seasons started to change after that, colder in the winter despite central heating, and sticky in the summer, despite the air conditioning. We sweated and fanned ourselves into adolescence, and worse: in 1970, boys I knew joined the cars driving north, and fathers woke to notes taped onto the refrigerator and one fewer pair of hands for the farming; or boys signed their names and went away and came home in caskets, or came home missing voices or limbs or minds. My mother held on to Ray, who was just young enough. Everything started to change. Years later, when I walked Jenny around the neighborhood in her stroller, whole fields were gone, including ours.

THE SNOW WAS gentle, thin, when it first started falling that morning in 1972. The forecast was for three inches, and I believed them.

I worked at the college library. I still do, though now I am a librarian. Back then, though, I sat behind the reserve desk, facing the dirty orange and red couches of the student lounge, and I sat for hours as the '72 storm began, hours before I realized how quiet the building was: no doors whining as another sweat-shirted student came inside; no dull thwacks as students threw open the reserve reading binders; no coughs or half-heard conversations or sneezes.

The overhead lights seemed dimmer suddenly, and in the cramped space behind the reserve desk, the air was stuffy. I took off my sweater. I put my book down and glanced at the clock. 1:00. For a moment I stood and listened. Then I knew why the library was hot. Nobody was opening the main doors and letting in the cool.

Even Myrna, my boss, had disappeared. She wasn't perched on her chair behind the counter at Circulation, nor did I hear the soft muttering to herself that usually gave her away. I walked to the main doors and looked out. I couldn't see across the lawn to the science building, a large, boxy modern monster out of sync with the staid brown stone buildings that made up most of the campus.

"Myrna?" My voice sounded loud to me.

Myrna was a Biology professor's wife. She seemed as ancient as the library itself. She was round and soft looking and known for her strawberry tarts. Several times a year, Professor Milligan walked into class carrying tin foil covered paper plates. He announced in a voice that sounded beleaguered and fatigued that yet again Mrs. Milligan had made too many tarts and soooo, before they discussed the topic at hand, would anyone like one? And he himself sat down in his tweed jacket and leaned his cane against the lectern and munched on a tart, or two. Or so I heard students say in their whispered conversations at the reserve reading desk.

It was Myrna who gave me my job. She had taken one look at my then slightly round belly and said: "I have someone who'll be leaving soon. A sit down job. That's what you want, right, a sit down job?" I'd nodded. Over the next several months, she patted me on the shoulder as my belly swelled, guided me to the bathroom when I was ill, poured over names in the baby naming books with me. Helen was too formal, Beatrice too British, Alice too soft sounding and weak. We chatted as we stamped books, lingered in the stacks behind Circulation to finish telling each other stories, or to start them. I told her, only her, how nervous I was, and she listened without interrupting me, without heaving big sighs and shaking her head, like my mother. Myrna said over and over again that the pain would be worth it. How lucky I was.

And once, just once, Myrna asked who he was, and I told her. He wore glasses with thick lenses and read late into the night, sitting by the window, reading by streetlight, so that I could sleep. He couldn't sleep. He paced like an alley cat and muttered to himself as he memorized. The pencils in his apartment were scarred with his tooth marks. He wanted to be a lawyer. He was studying for exams. He could not (didn't I see?) be a father. What was I thinking? he said, speaking to me with a pencil in his mouth, with his hands stuck between the pages of a book, marking his place.

Myrna came to visit the very day Jenny was born, and she often babysat so I could go out without bothering my mother, so that October morning, with a feeling of disquiet sweeping over me, I went looking for Myrna, whispering her name.

"Somebody has ripped off the sexual horoscope book again," she said. She stepped into the Circulation area with a sheaf of papers in her hands. "Did you call me?"

"Look."

We walked over to the main doors and stood side by side and stared at the storm. We could see nothing but snow.

"They haven't cancelled classes, have they?" she asked. "Is the elementary school out?"

"Not that I know of..." my voice trailed off. We had not had the radio on all morning. "Maybe I should call."

The superintendent then was the superintendent I had had when I was in school, and I knew he rarely canceled school, unless the depot door was frozen shut and the buses couldn't get out, or the weather threatened to stick him with schools full of kids overnight.

The school office took a long time to answer the phone, and I sat and listened to the static on the line cackle and hiss.

MOTHERLY

Someone finally picked up. Her voice was broken, coming to me in bits.

"Are you letting the elementary kids out?" I asked, but she couldn't hear, and I tried again, yelling this time, suddenly struck by the vision of my small five year old daughter standing on the sidewalk, unable to see for the snow.

"...out," the answer came.

I grabbed my sweater and purse and headed for the door, Myrna right behind me.

"How was I supposed to know this?"

But Myrna had no answers, never having had any children. The irony of the situation, a biology professor's sterile wife and me, fertile too early and too young, asking her for help.

But Myrna was motherly, and I had never had motherly in my life.

I HAD HAD a chance to go to college. Not here, but in the city. I didn't go. I couldn't make up my mind. Was a university for me? My parents said yes, even Ray said yes, but I twisted my hair around one finger and smoked cigarettes and considered my options. I thought I had options, though I'm not sure why. I had one chance, one scholarship. Too bad if I wanted bells to wake me in the morning and a college green and a Philosophy professor who still got lost on campus after teaching for twenty years (his excuse: they keep adding new buildings).

Take the scholarship, my mother said, thin-lipped. Take it. What are you waiting for? But I couldn't make myself call and say yes. The deadline to accept the scholarship passed, and my mother said, "Carol, that was stupid." I couldn't stay here with them all staring at me, shaking their heads, even Ray, in his jeans and sneakers and with a football under his arm like an appendage. I bought a ticket on Greyhound. In Chicago, too scared to think clearly, I switched buses and aimed for California. And then, well, life always takes funny turns. I came back in late July with one suitcase and a suntan and a blossoming belly.

In the fall, when the college kids came back from trips to Europe and summer jobs on the Cape and internships in Washington, DC., I sat at attention at my new job, eager to do one thing correctly. The library, quiet in the stifling days of August, was revived by the rush of energy. I woke up then, as if from my own hibernation, and handed out books on Martin Luther and the philosophy of science and the economics of the Civil War. And when the desk was slow, I grabbed a syllabus from an interesting course and followed along. Once a girl came to the desk, desperate for copy of a book which I could find nowhere, until I realized I had it. I handed the book to her and laughed a small laugh. She laughed, too, and then said: Are you in this class? I've never seen you there.

Every once in a while, I reached into the reserve test file

and took an essay exam. *Which is more threatening to the Greek Orthodox Church in the Soviet Union, Communism or apathy? Defend.*

I always gave myself an A.

THE CARS IN the library parking lot looked similar, with their thick coating of snow. I found my car by memory. I scraped off the necessary, put the windshield wipers on high, and drove at five miles an hour with my brights on, muttering to myself. I strained to see the road and occasionally I rolled my window down and swept the snow from the windshield myself. My car sputtered. I turned off my brights. I drove to the bus stop and sat in my car, lights aimed toward the road.

The bus appeared slowly, coming through the white haze in pieces, headlights first, then the bulky frame. The bus stopped, and the door swung open, and I watched numb with relief as the children filed off and the bus inched away. The larger kids slipped off into the storm, undaunted. I didn't think of calling Jenny's name. I grabbed children by the arms and pressed their faces near mine to see. Most squirmed away, but one didn't, and I looked and looked and knew she was Jenny.

"I was so worried about you," I said.

"Why?" she said.

"Because of all the snow. I worried you might get lost."

"I know how to get home," she said.

I held her hand as clumps of children headed off and got swallowed by the storm. A few cars came and picked up others. I got Jenny in the car and then I noticed a cluster of small children. I counted them. Six. I thought I could squeeze six little people into my car, but then my car sputtered again and wouldn't start. I paused and waited, but the car was dead and the snow came down and no other cars appeared and the road was a ghostly, crackling white expanse.

When we began to walk toward home, I waved to the others to join us, little ones whose hats slipped down to their noses and whose mittens had clips. I was furious. I wanted to know whose brilliant idea it was to send little kids home in a storm like this without anyone to meet them, and I wanted, more than anything, to know where the hell I was going. The street lights weren't coming on yet in the few sections of road that had them, and behind me came this passel of kids, silent and trusting and breaking in the cold. I looked for road signs, for fences, for anything that was familiar, but the selling of the land and the tearing down of the fences and the readjustment of property lines made it hard for me to tell where I was.

Circles, I thought.

I made the kids hold hands, and I felt like we were playing a giant game of crack the whip, with one small child on the far end swinging in the storm as we walked across what I was sure had once been farmland.

WHEN I CAME home from California, my mother opened the front door. I'd hoped Ray would be there and that I could squeeze past him before my mother really got a good look at me. But Mom threw the door open, as if she knew I was standing on the porch, and she saw my roundness and the way I stood with my hands on my hips, and we looked each other straight in the eye.

"Don't say a word," I said, brushing past her.

I heard the front door shut behind me, heard her footsteps behind mine. I picked up my pace, and she picked up hers, then I picked up mine, and she matched me. I stopped, hesitated, and she ran into me. My belly moved before any other part of my body, like my stomach was a balloon. I felt like I was floating outward and then down, until Mom grabbed me to keep me from falling. She wrapped her arms tightly around my shoulders, and her words came out hard and short and fast, like her breaths:

"Do you want this baby?"

"Yes."

"Do you?"

"Yes," and my voice sounded strangled to me.

She held on, and I tugged at her arms, repeating over and over, yes, yes, yes.

"Okay," she said, letting go. "All right."

I lifted my head and saw Ray standing at the top of the

stairs. What was left of my father leaned against the door jamb and gripped a breathing machine.

"Carol? What's going on?" My father wheezed out each word.

I stayed hunched over with my hands on my knees, and then slowly I stood. I didn't want to look at him, to see the loose skin and his gray scruff of a beard and the way he shuffled when he walked, at 45, but I stood, out of respect, out of some kind of odd recognition on my part that the worst thing, the most insulting thing I could do, would be to exclude him from his own family concerns; and so I raised myself up, and I let my hands fall to my sides, and before I could open my mouth, Ray opened his. He said: "Holy shit."

DURING THAT OCTOBER storm, I finally found an old battered fence, and we walked along the railings in single file, like a mother duck and her chicks. Suddenly Jenny stepped out of line and veered to the right.

"This is shorter."

"Jenny...-"

But already one or two little kids were trailing after her, lifting their feet high and sinking down into the soft snow, each one treading in the others' footsteps.

I watched her cutting across the field. I thought, how could she know when I don't?

WHEN I FIRST moved back from California, I refused to live with my parents. Later, after Dad died, I moved back home. But in the beginning I took the hourly job at the library and moved into a dank attic apartment not far from Mom and Dad's house and collected food stamps. Every day I picked a word from the dictionary and learned its meanings. *Demivolt, fusillade, Rosicrucian.* Several times a week Mom sent Ray over to get me in his muscle car, which rose high off the ground in the back. She had made a pot roast, and she had extra. Or stuffed green peppers. Or meat loaf, and each time I dropped by, Dad found an excuse to hand me a check.

Dad was as thin as the cigarettes he once smoked, and as he shrank, Ray expanded. Ray joined the football team and grew thick. He ate what my father could not eat, and later, when he stopped playing ball, he continued to eat like he was a linebacker, and he softened and rounded out and looked puffy-eyed and sallow.

After one breathless meal together, my father waved me over, and I pulled him to his feet and handed him the thin, cool metal tube attached to his Liberator. Mom stacked the dishes and brought them into the kitchen, and the faucet turned on with a groan. Ray disappeared; for all his bulk, he was stealthy.

Each word drained a reserve of effort and energy which

my father needed, and so as he began to speak, I leaned close to him and listened to the wispy sounding words, half-whistled, half-spoken, that were his new language.

"Who's going to help you?"

He must have seen the confusion in my face.

"In labor," he added, and then he sat back.

I knew what he wanted me to do. I looked at him, then looked away and listened to the clank and din of Mom washing the dishes. I thought of being in labor and having Mom there and wished the person would be Myrna, who talked to me about baby shoes and little hats, not where to find second hand clothing and how to mash up food into pulp. But my father's hand was rested on mine, like a feather, and I couldn't ignore the weightlessness of his hand, nor the weight of his request. The months I had yet to go were months in which he would linger like smoke, and he wanted my mother there with me to make sure, to make sure.

The next day I asked my mother to coach me, and when I gave birth to Jenny, my mother's hands were clenched in mine, and as I screamed, she screamed.

The doctor asked my mother to be quiet, but my mother shook her head no.

She said: "She needs me to scream, too."

And she was right. The force of my mother seemed to seep into me, and we roared Jenny into existence together.

JENNY STOPPED IN the middle of the field, looking from one side to the other, and that propelled me into action. The snow coming down and down and down had me panicked, and I loped after her, kicking snow into the air, onto myself, and calling her name. The children huddled together like frightened animals and waited for me, their eyes large and their little bodies quaking.

"Jenny!" I said, grabbing her hand. "Jenny."

"I know the way."

"Back to the fence!"

One child near Jenny took a tentative step forward, and I grabbed his hand with my free one and we marched. I felt like a drill sergeant.

"It's that way," Jenny said, pointing back.

"No, we're going to stick near the fence. If I'm right, it's old Carter's and we'll follow it home."

Jenny tugged free of my hand, and I felt the release, the sudden lightness. I reached out, but she moved around my hand, making her own way toward the fence.

We lined up, and my fingers felt like talons, frozen into curls ready to grip their hands in mine. One child was crying, and I ordered him not to cry. I yelled at them above a gust of wind, and the children stepped forward. I yelled for every parent whose child was with me, and for every parent who would call that damned superintendent in the morning, and for every parent whose child had, for the first time, pulled away.

My mother put two tea kettles on when we arrived. She unwrapped the children from their wet jackets and scarves and wrapped them back up in comforters and blankets. She learned their names, and she poured hot chocolate for them, and tried to crack jokes. She searched for their families in the phone book.

I sat at the kitchen table with my head in my hands.

"Now," my mother said, stopping briefly to touch my shoulder," are you all right?"

"What did I miss?"

"Nothing. It picked up speed, and I think they made a quick decision." My mother shrugged. "I got a call and tried to reach you, but Myrna said you had just left."

When I looked at her, she was busy again, searching for Kleenex for one of the kids.

"She pulled away from me," I said.

My mother rummaged in a drawer.

"She...-"

"I heard," Mom said.

She handed the child a Kleenex and then she would not look at me. She rested her hands on the sides of the drawer.

"She will pull away," my mother said. "And what you do is you hold on." She paused. "It's hard."

Maybe this was one reason my mother was strong. She

never let go. She seemed to be made of iron and steel and tree bark and stones. But suddenly I wondered, why did I remember only her toughest moments? I never doubted she loved me.

I got up and stood next to her, then placed my hand on her shoulder. Put your hand on mine, I thought. Please.

My mother didn't, but she leaned against me.

"You have to let go," my mother said, "but you always hold on."

As darkness came, headlights like moons slipped across our windows. Parents knocked on our door, blinking, and took their children away one by one, with a hand shake and a thank you and a word or two about the system for letting kids out during storms. Jenny clung to my mother, and I watched them stand in the doorway and wave good-bye together.

"Is this your daughter?" one woman asked.

My mother smiled, I imagine. At least, I have always imagined that she smiled when she said, "No. This is my grand-daughter."

Now the lights in the houses switch on slowly. It's dusk, and the few remaining skaters on the homemade ice rink turn into shadows. The radio turns to news. I hardly listen. I watch the shadows inch around the rink. I stare at what was once Carter's barn, Carter's house, Carter's field. I stare at what were once our fields.

I know some things. I know that I have ten toes and ten fingers and two hands. I know that I am not my mother, whose loneliness has a grit to it and helps her hold on. I know that I am made of paper and indices, bedtime stories and fairy houses, dark soil and silos—things that are passing away. I know that on Sundays the newspaper will have cartoons, and that I'll be able to call Jenny because the rates will go down. I know that when I call, she might be out, studying in the library or having coffee with a friend, all the things I hope she'll do. But I know how I will feel if she is not there, how a blackness will suddenly fill me, how I will feel full of holes, so many holes that the darkness leaves me as quickly as it comes. And then I will feel like air.

FISH EYES IN MOONLIGHT

THE HOUSE IS quiet now. John's weighty footsteps, followed by my granddaughter Elsa's snappy ones, followed by the low drone of their conversation as they descended the stairs: all this has passed. They walked by my bedroom reminding one another in hoarse whispers to be quiet. As if on cue, the protestations of this aged house temporarily subsided. No creaking floorboards or humming pipes mark the rituals of bedtime, no radiators hiss, no mysterious clicks and taps and squeaks punctuate the night. Without the racket, I lose sense of time. Normally they would be asleep now, Elsa and John; but tonight, like me, sleep has not yet saved them.

For a week, I have listened, strained to hear, the recurring nightly dialogue between Elsa and John. The ceiling between the study and my bedroom is thin, and when their voices rise, then hush, then rise again, I catch words. I piece sentence fragments together.

Tonight:

"How long can he go on like this?" John's voice is clear, almost loud.

Elsa mumbles an answer. There is a scraping sound as a chair is pushed backward across the hardwood floor.

I lie on crisp white sheets with a wool blanket pulled up to my chin. Whenever I shift my weight, the plastic underneath me crinkles. The sound reminds me: this room was meant to be a nursery. Even though I never saw it used as one, they described the room to me in such detail that I notice changes. The child size wooden chair with the cane seat is gone, as is the Children's Museum alphabet poster. The crib is in the attic, displaced by my bookcase and my scratched, mahogany wardrobe. The sailboat mobile, the stuffed bear, the light switch covers which said ON and OFF are gone.

What remains is Elsa's circus, which she painted along the uppermost edge of each white wall: elephants pirouetting on pale pink toe shoes; multi-colored fish whose eyes, because they are imitation glass, sparkle when struck by light; bears stretched out on their bellies, asleep; goats with horn-rimmed glasses bucking at the elephants, making them twirl.

Elsa apologized for the circus the day I arrived. She picked me up at my house on a crisp September day roughly a year ago and drove me around the city so that my departure was gradual. I whispered good-bye to the Charles, whispered good-bye to Fenway, though the stadium wasn't in view. We drove through Northampton, and I stared out the window at the college girls, who are now able to wear Bermuda shorts on campus. The leaves gave the valley a fiery look, with the red and brown and yellow saturating the hills, and as we drove off Route 9 onto the twisting, narrow hill roads, we were surrounded, overcome, by color.

In Lenox, we unloaded the station wagon. John was attending a conference at Princeton on al-Hallaj and al-Bistami, two Sufis from the fourth century or so who walked about town crying "al-Haqq," or "I am God."

Elsa heaved my suitcases from the back end of the wagon while I admired the house, a gray cottage with black shutters, a screened-in porch and gables. The lawn was a mixture of leaves and grass and sloped down to a stone fence, past which was the road. They had just bought the house in late July, for the baby who did not arrive. I had not seen the house before. As she slammed the back end shut, I thought, what a beautiful place to die.

Elsa, head bent, blonde hair falling in her eyes, carried my bags up the stairs, for even then I lacked strength. Yet so did she. Climbing the stairs was slow and tedious for us both. We rested on the landing, each of us flushed, laughing. Then she showed me my room. I glanced at her. She was twisting her mouth to the side, biting her lip. I put my arm around her shoulders, and we stepped, squeezed into the room together.

First I noticed my boxes, counted them. I counted them a second time. Then I noticed the hardwood floors, the two windows facing the road, with a view down the hill. Then on the wall I saw the glimmers, the glints, of light.

Elsa asked: "Granddad, can you bear it?"

I missed the pun. I remember staring at the fish eyes, at the pink toes of plump gray elephants. I tried to imagine sitting among them, at age 82, smoking my pipe and reading Churchill biographies or Nabokov or Patrick O'Brien. I walked farther into the room and turned slowly on my heels, slowly so I wouldn't fall, and stared in disbelief at the animal parade.

No, I said at length.

Elsa was silent.

When did you do this? I asked.

After, she replied. In August.

Yet over the year, I grew fond of the animals, especially the elephants on point. Now, they are company. Tonight, in the darkness, the elephants are impossible to distinguish. Tonight I see the flash of fish eyes in moonlight. The moon is a fall moon, round and hazy and pale. Above the trees, the moon is haunting. Its presence adds to the chill in the air.

I am propped into a sitting position by a stack of pillows.

I cannot sleep like this, but Elsa and John are afraid that if the pillows are removed, I will slip away one night. I don't want the pillows; they insist. I didn't want to meet with a second heart specialist last April for another opinion, yet I was bundled into the station wagon and driven to his office in Boston, only to be told again that no more could be done for me, that I might even linger indefinitely. I hardly cared to meet the local flower club, but they arrived en masse one day and sucked me into a conversation on regional wildflowers. I don't enjoy my evenings alone. I don't enjoy my meals on a tray, without company.

Life wasn't always like this.

I remember the days before their nighttime discussions began, the days before last March, the days before last April: days of Indian summer, full of heat and light and the dizzying fragrance of our garden lilacs. We ate picnic lunches out of wicker baskets crammed with apples and slices of beef, Camembert, baguettes, and bottles of Pinot Grigio. We threw windows open to catch breezes and birdsong. We watched sunsets, brilliant, moody orchestrations, intensified by age and reflection and a glass of wine. And on humid nights, when the lilac scent overpowered and the world about me dozed, I kicked off my sheets and leaned on the window sill. I stared up at the stars and was young. My wrinkled hands, my achy back: these were not of my body. My mind was the same mind, my soul the same soul, but my body was a body I did not know.

Our winter days were short-lived, gray, and damp. Weekdays we separated at breakfast, gathered together at dinner. Saturdays, but especially Sundays, we shared in our own way, me in the living room, Elsa in the den, John in the kitchen. I still hear the clipped pace of Elsa's fingertips across the keyboard, and John's droning voice as he practiced his lectures. I bundled up in the afghan and listened as Elsa read her chapter out loud to herself and thereby taught me about hermeneutics, or as John discussed the relevance of Sufism to Islam and quoted Rumi.

I, who was not a scholar, reveled in their life of the mind, in the ease with which they grasped complexity; was awed by their knitted brows and by the way, on the rarest of rare days, an idea or realization froze them mid-sentence, caused them to catch their breath, until suddenly, suddenly, they raced to the typewriter, or to one another, and the house came alive, as if shaken by a force greater than love or fear or guilt.

They explained their discoveries to me, looked me in the eye, slowed their speech, and enunciated each word, though I heard them perfectly. Elsa, looking much like her father, earnestly stared at me: "Granddad, listen to what I wrote." This I remember most clearly: their hands in mine, their faces alight, the glow of which made me, if only momentarily, warm.

On Sunday nights in winter, John would build a fire. As those evenings wore on and the fire dimmed, we became storytellers. John spoke of visits to Cairo and the advice his father gave him on teaching and the high-backed chair in which his grandfather used to read; and Elsa, of apple-picking trips with her mother and the day she first loved John and weekends with her grandmother and me. And I spoke as well, though my voice lacked force.

Above the hiss of the fire I told them of family long dead and the garden I roamed as a child, my first car, an Oldsmobile, and the late late night when my commanding officer came to me and said my son, Elsa's father, was dead. I spoke of times both bleak and horrible which, though history to them, yet resonate for me: my first years at sea, commanding a landing barge when we stormed the Normandy beaches, and twenty years after retiring, finding Edward's name carved into the far left panel of the Vietnam War Memorial, one name among many but the only one I loved; and weeping, with my head to the cool, inanimate marble, weeping beside other men and women and in front of children, who watched as we laid to rest our ghosts, strangers all, yet connected.

Those days and nights were without equal, and we knew then they would not last. Each memory is like a pointillist painting, blurry at first glance, then coarse in detail. In each memory I am more gaunt, and they, according to their degree of determination, more animated or less.

On nights like tonight, I am alone. I hardly see them now.

Their days are of full of school; their nights are full of talk. As if they can save my life with words, save my life at all. My heart valve does not work.

I am an old man, a thin, frail old man who is passionate about gardens, Auden, Pavarotti, and the sea. I am not ready to leave. I try to explain to Elsa and John that I am not dying as a system, all sinking fast at once. I am going in pieces. My capabilities diminish in increments. The tragedy is that once I planted the garden with daisies, roses, portulaca, rhododendron bushes. I attended concerts at Tanglewood, frequented the bookstores, joined their dinner parties. The tragedy is in the contrast.

Now a nurse visits me twice a week. I stay in bed because walking drains me. Speaking is a struggle, and I drool. I cannot catch my breath and gasp like a fish in stagnant water. I am betrayed. I am the old man who occasionally forgot to turn off the stove. I am the old man who, weathered by age and illness and sea winds, has grown thin and unrecognizable. I am the child they decided to wait to have.

They wanted me with them. Insisted. No nursing home. Sell the house, John said, move in with us. I hesitated; they called again. I warned them: Age is without mercy.

No one is prepared for this.

Last March at Mass. General, the surgeon told me I needed valve replacement surgery. A valve in my heart. He informed me that an artificial valve was available, but a pig valve would be more natural. However, he said, pig valves only last ten years, whereas an artificial valve could last for twenty.

I said to him: I don't want to have to go through this again in ten years, but let's keep me as natural as possible. Give me the pig.

X-rays. Tests. White coats and the rumble of wheels along tile. Hours spent under the sickly yellow glow of fluorescent lights.

I shared my hospital room with another man, a man who was older than me but looked younger. He was not bald; his hair was gray. He, too, was in need of a pig valve. His operation went smoothly, and when he woke up, came out of the fog, he turned to his daughter and said oink. I laughed. Elsa laughed. But John, who came in from the corridor, smiled a thin, tense smile. The doctor had just told him I could not have a pig or any valve. With my hardened arteries and my kidney problems, surgery was too much of a risk. I was stunned: I failed to qualify for a pig valve.

John said, softly, which somehow hit me harder than if he'd bellowed: Granddad, we're taking you home.

John and Elsa consult me: does my medicine help? Do I have any letters to write? Do I want a service? I wonder if rituals matter, if I could go without them. My words are slurred, incomprehensible, and they bend down to hear me. I answer: I am too tired. You decide.

I know this is not fair.

Before I came to live with them, they traveled to Mecca, to Cairo, to Berlin. They gave papers, then dashed off to explore. She frequently wrote letters to share their adventures: "Dearest Granddad, I am writing from the balcony overlooking the sea...Next we are off to Alexandria with our papers and pens." John invariably signed them and added his own scribble: "The Mediterranean is beautiful. I dream in Arabic here."

This year, they are taking care of me.

I'm tired of battling myself to breathe. Each breath is rasping, and I am suddenly sick of life. Yet I know myself well. I know that I don't think I'll ever really die. Spirit persists. Must persist. I am ready. I am not ready. I am as ready, as reconciled to the inevitable, as I will ever be. To hell with pillows, to hell with ritual. To hell with each rasping breath.

I drift to my wedding day and to Janey, to the softness in her eyes when she smiled at me, to the morning I awoke and she did not, to Edward. Edward sitting on Janey's lap, singing Little Drummer Boy out of tune. Edward, tow-headed and nimble, racing to victory for the fourth grade. Edward and Monie and then Elsa, whom he never knew. He was an advisor to the Vietnamese Air Force, killed at Pleiku in 1959. One of the first to not come home.

I paid my respects. In 1984 I made the trip to Washington with Janey, who was thin lipped and peaked. I touched the letters of his name. Janey made a rubbing. With effort, I walked the length of the Memorial. I was reminded then, as I walked beside that marble wall, of an earlier visit to pay my respects, of Omaha Beach and the field of white crosses. A white cross for each identifiable body. Of boys I had known. In Washington D.C., there was no cross for Edward.

Scattered, my thoughts become scattered. My memory is disordered, out of sequence. I cannot imagine not being. I cannot imagine nothingness.

School began this month. Elsa's book is due out. John is a guest lecturer in a class on the Crusades. Providing the other point of view, he says. He is also teaching a course on Islam, in which he has nine students. The nine smartest, he is sure. He is not like Elsa, who looks above the heads of the students when she lectures and who, when giving papers at conferences, brings a glass to the podium, not of water, but of vodka. John thrives on having an audience. When he took a sabbatical from Amherst last year, Elsa said he was impossible.

Tonight is not too distant from that other fall night, roughly a year ago, when this became my home. Tonight is not too distant from any night, any day. Why do I remember this? John returned from his Sufism conference that night, while I was unpacking. I heard him before I saw him, waited for him to appear.

"Welcome, Granddad," he said, stepping in the room to hug me. "I'm glad you're here. Good trip?"

"Yes. How is al-Bistami?"

"Ecstatic."

Then he retreated to the doorjamb and watched me count my books, count again. He walked over to the window, opened it, leaned on the sill, stuck his head outside.

"Elsa says you're a little unsure about living with a bunch of gleaming fish eyes and pirouetting elephants."

I laughed, shrugged. "I'm an old man, John. Gleaming fish eyes..." My voice trailed off. "I'd never ask you to get rid of the animal parade." I paused. "You know, it's not too late to try again."

"No." His voice sounded tentative.

I looked at my books. I could not count, lost count, suddenly didn't give a damn.

"We waited too long to start. We learned too late we would have problems. Conceiving, maintaining." He put his face in his hands. "I'll never forget the look on her face."

A breeze. I sat down on a stack of books.

"We named him Edward, after both of you. Edward John. Did we tell you that?" He leaned out the window for several minutes, then shook his head fiercely. When he stepped back into the room, there was a smile on his face. "A drink?"

"I never turn one down."

He left, returning almost immediately with a bottle of wine

and two glasses. He poured. We turned off the lights and sat, silently, waiting for moonlight to hit the wall.

I have not had a drink with him for weeks. He no longer offers. Yesterday I asked for a glass of white wine. The thought of sitting in bed with a glass of chardonnay, under moonlit fish eyes, appealed to me. Elsa said no. She was inflexible. No more alcohol.

Every evening Elsa kisses me goodnight and says, " I love you, Granddad." John reads the paper to me, tells me how the flowers look. He tells me about the Red Sox, and we have a few seconds of silence with God on the team's behalf. Sometimes I recall days from my childhood, but John becomes quiet, contemplative. He squeezes my hand. But these are only minutes in long days. I miss their letters, which were long conversations continued by post. I miss summer picnics and winter Sundays. I miss the celebration of ideas as they thunder into existence on cold, wet days in Lenox.

This will be, one night, the time allotted to me, this time between a goodnight kiss and the baseball scores. All I will have will be that moment of silence before they leave, before I leave.

Now, night and I are company again. Elsa and John whisper, or not. Their voices succumb to fatigue; the beast with which they wrestled is put to bed. In the stillness, I recall her letters, the picnics, the fireside conversations. Not long ago she said to me, mid-way through a wheeling across the garden on our last warm summer day, of this summer, my last, and she said that no trip was worth missing me, no paper or lecture or luncheon or tea. She needed to tell me, and she spoke for them both, that I am not a burden.

I wonder what I will miss of seasons to come. I cannot bear to miss anything.

The slapslapslap of footsteps. Elsa's. Then:

"...have that new priest over...St. Andrew's?" John again.

Clinking, as ice smacks against glass. Elsa's voice becomes shrill.

"We should at least ask him." John, sounding tired.

I search in the darkness for the animal parade, for the elephants with pink toes and goats with glasses and the bears who slumber, never waking. I cannot see them. In the moonlight, I see only gleaming fish eyes.

Suddenly, the house groans, settles, clicks, is silent yet again. I wait to hear a squeaking door or footfall or the whoosh of curtains roused by wind. The quiet persists. In the stillness, it is my turn to speak; and word by word, emotion by emotion, till all is said and there is nothing left to say, till silence looms and darkness is a comfort, I speak. In this room that is my last room I practice my good-byes.

TAKING ROOT

A L HAD THE porch light on against the dark. In this old neighborhood, street lights were few and far between, with just enough illumination to spare accidents and discourage some trouble, but tonight he wanted more, as a comfort to himself, and as a guide.

This late, the neighborhood was quiet, just the occasional breeze whispering through the solemn row of Russian olives at the bottom of his sloping lawn, down near the sidewalk. The sound eased him, seemed to shhh away his worries. He had expected more sound this evening, the lilt of voices in a passing conversation or, in this neighborhood, the thud and backfire of anybody's car. But as Sunday slipped into Monday, it did so with a whisper.

Next to him, Al heard Marshall's collar jingle as he shifted weight in his sleep. Marshall was an old dog. He wasn't even Al and Sarah's old dog, but here he was, as always, right beside Al. Marshall was a beautiful golden retriever with a flourish of a tail and large brown, rheumy eyes, and he was besotted with Al for reasons no one fully understood. Their next door neighbor, Mark, took the betrayal with good grace. Al felt grateful. Mildly anxious, but grateful. He knew, and he knew that Marshall knew, how much he needed one solid, reliable friend. Maybe loneliness was recognizable. Maybe it had a scent.

They were an odd collection, this clutch of neighbors. Mark, who shared Marshall with Al and Sarah and their one small child, only one; Howard and Norda across the street, serial hosts; and Anil, who lived next door to Howard and Norda and who seemed to have enough children for them all, enough to bust the seams of his house. It was clear the seams of Anil's budget were straining. Wasn't it Meira who had appeared the other day in a parka a size or two too small? Al tried, as circumstance allowed, to slip small kindnesses Anil's way, little gestures he hoped nobody noticed. Occasionally Al and Sarah watched the children, helped with rides, shared meals. But for all the kindnesses among them—hell, he and Mark even shared a dog—there was a reserve, a thin line. In this age of confession, they kept much to themselves.

The glow from the street lights caught Howard's rusting bucket of a Chevy across the street, not to be outdone by Mark's dented bucket of a Tempo next door, and farther down the road, Anil's Volvo. They had a bet running, the whole block, on which would go first. Even Howard, Mark, and Anil had weighed in. Al had voted for Mark's Tempo. He knew that Howard had recently reworked the Chevy's engine. And Anil. Poor Anil. He would keep that Volvo running if only with prayer. He had nothing to spare for additional expenses.

Sometime soon, out from the pitch black night, would come Sarah's Volkswagon. They had been gone a week, his girls. Al couldn't quite sit still now. Any minute, there would be that familiar throaty thrum, that flash of headlights, and then, finally, there would be his wife and young daughter, who knew how tired, who knew how transformed, but home nonetheless because this *was* home, this ancient house and the property line of Russian olives, with the old dog that was not theirs, and Al.

His heart was entirely theirs.

In this neighborhood of unreliable cars and steady, hopeful hearts. In this city known for its winters, in the middle of the plains, in the heart of the country. In this gentle summer soon to slip into the crisp cool of fall. Here in some kind of broken down glory, they had taken root, and thrived. Mostly.

Now Al rose and stood at the porch rail, tapping his fingers, and finally, with a low groan, Marshall joined him standing, and they waited together in the long, long night for the be-ginning, for sight of those headlights. For the welcoming home.

LEAVING WAS SARAH's idea. Leaving, she had made clear, in no way meant that she was leaving forever, or even un-happy. She was only tired and in a rut. She wanted to get away. She would have preferred to leave Amelia with Al and go off somewhere by herself, even to someplace like a monas-tery. Instead, Sarah chose a quiet New Mexico town, a small, sleepy place where she and Amelia could linger on the cheap and have some adventures, shop in the cozy downtown, have some lunches out, take hikes in the low, long hills. Be left alone and tourist free.

Al understood. He felt a bit panicked, but he did under-stand. The panic came from her clear assertion, her looking away as she said it, that she didn't know when they would be back.

"Are you thinking two weeks?" he had laughed nervously. "Or two months?'

Sarah had shrugged, her blonde hair slipping behind her bony shoulders. Sarah had grown as thin as her sister, Glennie. Neither sister was tall, and they had tiny frames, but Sarah had always carried enough weight to look strong. Glennie had only ever been a string bean with flowing, gorgeous golden hair. The weight of Glennie's hair, he was sure, rivaled her body weight. But now here was Sarah as tiny, and after all their years of worrying about Glennie, now Al worried for Sarah. He worried for his bright-eyed Amelia. He almost said, "Leave her here," but he knew Amelia would be confused, and he knew, too, that without Amelia Sarah would lose an anchor. Her focus.

"Take what time you need," Al had said. "I'll have Marshall," he added with a laugh, and at this last, Sarah had tipped her head and squinted at him, smiling slightly.

"This scares me to death, Sarah," he finally said.

That was when she said it wasn't over. It wasn't about them. It was some restlessness in her that she needed to put to rest, a fatigue. Al let it go. Despite the dissipating tension, pressing her for information or details felt dangerous. They were standing in the kitchen in the buttery glow of morning, the sun warming the yellow walls just as they'd planned when, newly married, they had chosen this home. Chosen it for this room and what light they could imagine. They knew the center of their world would be their kitchen. Seven years now, and one rambunctious four-year-old later, here they stood.

"Part of it is the miscarriage," Sarah had said.

Al watched her, saw her face twitch. He could not know her grief. He knew part of it, but he did not know how it felt for that beautiful hope to slide, then wrestle its way out of her. *Let it go naturally*, the doctor had said, and they had all agreed. Natural sounded good, preferable. But Al had been angry ever since. Had he known it was a lengthy process. Had he known what pain Sarah would feel, that she'd be keening, rocking on the bedroom floor at one point and grasping his hands, he would have suggested exploring alternatives. She had needed a gentler passing. They both had. They had choked out a farewell to the baby that late haunted night and far later, when they had had the strength, they had planted a small tree for the heart they would never know. A silver maple. Something strong and proud. Not like the Russian olives, with their gray green leaves and sad bending branches.

That terrible night as he had held her and whispered careful soft assurances, Sarah had said to him. "I bet in heaven I'll see some tiny angel and will know its face."

Al hadn't shared her hope in this future reunion. He wasn't religious, though he was a religion professor. But the idea took root once she left on her road trip with Amelia, and he began to think that perhaps there was a heaven and that up there, in the back row, the tiniest voice in the choir was his child, singing and laughing and waiting. It was silly. "Absolutely silly," he told himself, each time the thought crossed his mind, but the thought stayed with him, a solace. He thought often about his child. He wondered if it had been a boy or girl. He wondered why the baby hadn't made it. He wondered why he couldn't quite escape the sharp grip of grief. It was always there, a thin, sliver of cold; a splinter. Something hair thin, like a small crack, something pointed that caught in him and created a widespread ache. Sometimes, Al had to stop and catch his breath.

JUST AFTER SARAH and Amelia had left, waving from their windows as the Volkswagen turned the corner and disappeared, Al took his coffee out on the porch. It, too, was a Sunday. The morning was cool, one of those late summer days that presaged fall. Al was ready. It was football season, and down the block he watched as Anil's oldest son, Sujay, gathered his gear and plonked it in the back of Anil's clunker.

"You have Sunday practice?" Al asked as they made their loud, slow progress down the street.

Their Volvo needed a new muffler, and the engine whirred as though going 15 miles an hour was straining all systems. Anil replied, but it was impossible to hear him over the noise.

Al waved them on and sat waiting for two things, a direction and the arrival of Marshall, who even now, having had a romp at the dog park with Mark, was making his way briskly up the cracked and heaving sidewalk toward Al, nose high. In the morning, first thing, Marshall had all the energy of a puppy.

"I've never had that, ever," thought Al.

Marshall settled himself on the porch after getting a

vigorous head rub and hearty greeting, the combination of which seemed key to his having a successful day and quite enough to ensure one, as long as Al then stayed nearby.

Across the street, the detritus of Howard and Norda's last late gathering lay gathered neatly by the garage. A stack of empty glass bottles in a variety of shapes and colors and a compacted though bulging dark green garbage sack.

What Al had not expected was to see a dapper looking Howard step out of the house and come across the lawn toward him. For a long moment, he couldn't speak, his thoughts gathering only slowly across the idea that he was not dapper. And not even fully awake.

"Al," said Howard. He looked a little gray, and Al felt secretly relieved to know Howard was human, and that he, Al, scruffy-faced with a significant paunch and a thatch of unruly hair sprouting from his head, was just one of the guys. Sort of.

"Hi, Howard."

How Howard and Norda maintained any semblance of a decent life, he had no idea, not with the racket they made each night, the parties. He imagined that at some point, they would crash, unable to keep up the pace. Parties and work and parties again. Crazy and reckless as they were, they had good hearts. Howard wouldn't blink before speeding across the street if he thought Al and Sarah needed him. Nor would Norda.

Tomorrow morning, as Al gathered his briefcase and student papers, that new textbook from Macmillan, his coat, he'd venture out to lecture looking every bit his age, and like a sad, worn out shoe: soft, weathered, maybe lovable. And there would be Norda in her sleek suit and high heels, and Howard in his brand name casuals, and off they'd go in Norda's little roadster, coffee in hand, smiles on their faces, looking crisp. They probably even smelled good up close, of a simple, fresh soap. They were a magazine cover. An ad.

If Howard and Norda were a manicured, landscaped yard, then Al and Sarah were an unmowed lawn. Slightly ruffled, wearing clothes with stains. They were also parents, something Al doubted that Howard and Norda could ever be and perhaps did not want. But what did he know? If he had learned anything recently, it was that one never knew another person's heart, not really. He had not known Sarah yearned for another child. He had not known how broken-hearted he'd feel at their loss, or how alone, in this place where there was no one to talk to save for Sarah, who barely had any words left herself, grief having somehow stolen her vocabulary. How often had she opened her mouth, then shook her head, unable to express herself?

But here was Howard, in pressed brown pants, his t-shirt unwrinkled, a pale blue like a bird's egg. Some fancy flip-flops.

"Did you need some help with something?" Al asked.

"How you holding up?"

Al smiled. "Been a bit lonely," he said, opting for honesty.

Howard's smile faded. "I'm sorry, Al. You're welcome…" he said, gesturing broadly at his house, at the carefully packaged garbage.

"Thanks, Howard. Very kind. But poor Marshall here might go into a decline alone."

Howard paused. He was standing in the front walk, a respectful early morning distance from where Al was on the porch.

"I feel a bit awkward." Howard couldn't look at Al.

That's when Al knew. The miscarriage had never been a secret. Not that he and Sarah had shared much with people, but it was hard not to let the news filter out. Sarah had sunk so low with the news of the impending loss, and they had needed some short notice help several times. The evening—that dark evening—when Sarah was hunched on the bathroom floor, weeping, Al had called Norda, who was closest, and she had come and stayed near Amelia's room in case she woke. Amelia loved Norda—her hats and flowing, flowery scarves; the hodgepodge of perfume bottles in her bedroom; her make-up kit, like a coloring box. Once Norda had let her try a bright red lipstick. Amelia fell in love then. With Norda. With lipstick. With the heady power of being a woman.

"It's wonderful news," Al said. "I'm sincerely happy for you." And he was. He felt something catch, took a moment to get air, but at the same time he felt genuinely pleased for

Norda and Howard. "I didn't realize you wanted children. It's the most special thing."

Howard smiled, his face lighter, a wash of joy coming over him. "We didn't plan it," he said. "But we're thrilled."

"Well, let us know if we can help with anything." The more he spoke, the more inadequate Al felt, as though he was speaking lines he had heard somewhere, from a book about how to handle awkward occasions, for instance.

"Actually, that's why I'm here," he said. "Norda isn't feeling well, and I think I should run her in. Our car is dead. That new engine. I am not sure what I did…" Howard's voice trailed off. "I was hoping you could run us down to urgent care."

"Of course," Al said, standing quickly. He cinched his robe around himself. "Give me a few minutes and I'll pull the car around."

Marshall whined, his eyes moving between the men, the air seeming suddenly electric, even to Al.

Later, Al worried as he waited in the car, engine running. Had Norda slept enough? Were people smoking in the house? Was Norda drinking? But it wasn't his business. Norda, though she needed help and looked drawn, managed to get out the door and down the steps. He couldn't see any belly on her, but she was tall and wouldn't show yet, he supposed.

Howard gently guided her into the backseat and as she settled, Norda flashed Al a wan smile. "Thanks for this, Al."

"Of course, Norda. Absolutely."

Howard had hardly settled in to the car himself before Al pulled away from the curb.

The car fell quiet. Norda had closed her eyes and let her head fall against the door, and every question Al thought to ask focused on the baby and asking anything now seemed inappropriate. He remembered too well the inadvertent wrong questions from kind-hearted neighbors and colleagues after the miscarriage, and he remembered the blessed, even tight-lipped silence from family, who seemed to know when to speak and when not.

Glennie, of course, had proven particularly helpful. After Sarah first got the news, and Al had been pulled out of class, he had dialed Glennie as he hurried to his car. Being as large as he was, he didn't move smoothly or with ease and he had wished for a stout heart to get him the speed he needed and to give him the courage he lacked.

Glennie had taken the call, a stunner. Her middle name was Unavailable.

"Hey, Al," she had said, and he couldn't speak. Then: "Is it Sarah or Amelia?"

"Sarah," he had gasped. "They just told her the baby is dead."

There was a pause. Glennie had not known about the baby. At that point, no one had. "Where is she?"

"Abbot Northwestern."

"I'll meet you there. Al, I am so sorry."

So sorry. Perhaps the kindest words he had ever heard from Glennie, who kept emotions in a special place to which he seemed denied access. She was always cool, in control. He wondered when she broke down and with whom. She had to cry sometime. Didn't she? Not even Sarah really knew.

Of course Glennie had gotten there before Al. Glennie, rail thin and with that gush of hair, that porcelain skin. Perfect complexion and perfectly composed, stood outside Sarah's door. Dr. Glennie MacMillan, OB GYN.

"She should see you first," Glennie said.

Of course she should. Seeing Glennie might not calm her right now.

But as Al opened the door, Glennie placed her hand on his shoulder and squeezed. He looked at her, and there were tears in her eyes. He stopped. For an instant, he stopped flat. He squeezed her hand back and then plowed through the door to that newly frail girl in the room who held his entire world in her hands.

At Abbott Northwestern now, again, Al parked the car by the doors and stood ready to help Howard get Norda out, but he wasn't needed, and he felt like a large flightless bird, flapping nearby. Then he had the sense to lumber ahead and secure a wheelchair.

Howard nodded, said "Thanks so much, Al."

After he parked, Al looked for them in the waiting room, but they weren't there, despite the crowd, and Al's heart rate picked up. He approached the front desk. "The pregnant couple?" he asked.

The receptionist, a plump young woman with a stylish bob, eyed him. "Family?"

"Friend. I drove them here."

The woman didn't speak right away, but she pushed back her chair from her desk and said a few words to a colleague around the corner, in the hall.

"They've sent her to emergency," the woman said. "Do you need directions?"

"It didn't seem urgent," Al said.

The woman's expression dimmed. She looked away. He knew she wasn't allowed to share more.

"I know the way," he said. He knew it all too well. How many visits had he made here for Sarah's grandparents? An endless number. And then for Sarah. He turned out of urgent care and began the walk he now hated.

IF WINTER WAS Sarah's season, fall was Al's. He loved crunching leaves underfoot, football (any football, though he bled gold and maroon for the Gophers), and all the holidays. He decorated the house for each of them in turn, and though he was a natural fit, he never offered to play Santa. He far preferred to be a part of the crowd than its star, to see Amelia's face light up, to be there with her. With them all.

Christmas was the one time each year he felt a glimmer of faith. Neighbors would pass a cup of cheer with a hearty, "This must be your season!" Al would chuckle and raise his glass. But if the season was his, it wasn't for the reasons they expected. He wasn't a religious man, just a Professor of Religion. He wasn't Santa. He was, he realized, a simple man. A happy, simple, quiet man.

Losing a child hadn't fit in to his worldview. It fit no one's, of course, but Al had been singularly unprepared for any loss. He asked for little, and he had been unmoored by the unnatural goodbye, by his insistent grief. And angry. Al had been angry.

Now he sat in a hard plastic chair, flipping through travel magazines and health brochures, waiting. Hoping. Because who would wish ill on a child? He needed, he realized, for this little baby to live. A new loss would unravel him. The thought struck him cold. He understood Sarah's leaving now in a new way. Suddenly he wanted to escape as well.

Across from him, an older man twisted his health brochure endlessly, his mouth a tight line, his knobby knuckles achingly large. An Hispanic family clumped together, heads down, praying. A middle aged man in a pinstripe suit paced. Al sat. He slumped down into himself. He closed his eyes. He tried hard to think good thoughts.

It was a while before Howard appeared. He looked drawn and tight, and Al's heart skipped a beat.

"You don't need to stay, Al. I just wanted to let you know that they're running some tests."

"I can stay, Howard. Can I get you anything?"

Howard shook his head. Then he said, abruptly. "Isn't your sister-in-law an OB?"

"Yes, she is. I'd be happy to call her, or to give you her number."

"Would you do both?"

Al dialed hurriedly, his thick fingers fumbling over the numbers. He had to redial. He left her a message. "Glennie, a friend of mine and Sarah's is here at the hospital. Howard and Norda. Norda is pregnant and there is a problem. Howard was wondering, I guess, if you could call him."

It was a miracle born from a painful place, a thread of memory, that allowed Al to remember and recite Howard's cell phone number, his voice sounding wooden. Howard, who sometimes worked from home, had been the person Al phoned from work for check-ins after their loss. *How is Sarah? Have you seen her?* But only once or twice, after those awful few days, and only until Sarah's mother moved from across town and took over.

Howard nodded a thank you, turned quickly and left, tears coming into his eyes. Al couldn't imagine. Yes he could.

It was not long before Al saw Glennie striding across the ER waiting room, that white coat flapping like a flag. She did not look for him, but she caught his eye once, as she turned before going in to the care area. She saw him then and lifted her hand. Once. As though he were a casual acquaintance, maybe a Resident. Then she was gone.

Glennie had been voted one of the top ten OB doctors in Minneapolis-St. Paul. She was featured in *Minnesota Monthly*. Her photo made her look like a goddess. Her honors and credentials were as lengthy as she was tall. And she was single, an absent aunt, a sometimes sister, an elusive personality with a ready, brief smile and a calm voice. Her hands never shook. Not like Al, who was shaking now. Shaking because he knew that one did not call Dr. Glennie MacMillan for anything routine. One called Glennie because a life depended on it. Thanks to *Minnesota Monthly*, everyone knew that. Everyone.

IN THE DAYS before Amelia, Sarah and Al had said many goodbyes to loved ones. Both of her grandparents, her Auntie Em. His grandfather, a stoic Scandinavian named Anders Anderson. *Not even Lars*, Al used to say. It was like naming someone Andrew Andrews.

But practice didn't make Al perfect. Every loss was harder to bear, the accumulation of absences loud and unsettling, accentuated by the strain between Sarah and Glennie, which had been going on for so long now it ought to have worn itself out. But wounds like theirs strengthen, Al had learned, in the face of passivity. The most recent goodbye—theirs, the child he always remembered as sound, that thumping, persistent heartbeat—had seemed to allow the sisters to drift closer, which he registered but couldn't absorb.

Sarah remembered other sounds, she had told him—the steady almost determined breathing of the tech, the squish of more jelly across her stomach, the clickclickclick of the tech taking picture after picture. Suddenly she had realized that the tech was searching. Then she caught the tech's glance and knew. She just knew. Sarah remembered the sound of her own loud breathing.

Glennie soon left the ER, her speed walk taking her past Al without a glance. He found himself bowing his head, toward what and for what he couldn't say, all of him suddenly feeling vacuumed out from his core. He bowed, head to hands, hands clasped on knees. He bowed down.

He was interested in faith, always had been, of course. Interested in the hope and calm it provided certain family and friends. Interested in how the ritual and beliefs had shaped his parents cold marriage. Al had always thought his parents lacked passion. He doubted they even liked each other, but lately, perhaps given his own aging, he realized they had some bond he had not given any credence before. They relied on each other, trusted each other. They had committed to each other and that came in part from faith.

But he never doubted the reasons he was an only child.

Now he searched his mind for the words that had defined his childhood, the prayer as important to the weave of his days once as lutefisk and football and books. But what he thought was far simpler. *Dear Lord, please protect the babies.*

Plural.

And then Al began to weep.

IT WAS LATE when they drove home. The neighborhood streetlights flickered. Al helped Howard bring Norda inside, settle her on the couch. He put a meal together, a green salad, bread and butter, some pasta, and left it on the table. He made Howard a drink. Then Al left, quietly closing the front door behind him.

Howard had said only that they believed the baby was all right. That, and thank you. The ride home had been tense, Norda curling in to Howard, who sat in the back, eyes wide open and unblinking. Al tried not to glance back at them. It seemed impossible.

On the front porch, Marshall stood and greeted Al, his tail wagging gently, his whine short and high pitched.

"I don't know, Marshall. I don't know if it's okay."

Inside, he put some food in Marshall's bowl and some

fresh water in a large clear Tupperware container, and then he lay down in bed, hoping to sleep forever. When Marshall curled in a ball near his feet, Al didn't protest. As Marshall inched his way closer to Al and stretched out, Al said nothing. He didn't care about rules and being sanitary and dog hair. Who gave a shit.

He thought of Sarah and Amelia. They have only been gone one day, Al thought.

One.

He checked the messages. No blinking light, just the steady red glare of a button. They were on the road, they were slipping through the dark, as was he. He felt as cracked open as an egg. Al thought he might stop breathing, and when he cried out, what rose out of him was loud, and raw, almost a scream, and then it became one. Marshall, beside him, whimpered. The women had each other, God, doctors, nurses. Who did the men have? What were their words for this particular grief?

Later that night, Al woke and went out onto the front porch. He was still wearing his clothes. He had not eaten. Across the street, Norda and Howard's house was silent, without lights. The trio of beaters lined the curb, looking, if possible, more forlorn. The streetlights glowed steadily now, dimly but steady.

Marshall followed Al outside, keeping close, pressing his frame against Al and steadying both of them.

Al looked up at the stars. *Dear Lord, please protect the babies*, he said in a whisper. Then he repeated it, over and over.

AL WAS ASLEEP on the porch when dawn broke. Sujay touched him lightly on the shoulder as he delivered the paper.

"You okay? Mr. Nelson?"

Al had nodded, tried to make himself presentable and to pretend that no, he was not asleep in his clothes on the front porch, next to a dog, even if it was Marshall.

"Want me to call someone?" Sujay asked. He glanced down the street toward his own home, already dialing.

It was the last thing Al needed.

"I'm fine, Sujay," Al said. "Fine, thanks. Please don't call anyone."

Sujay hesitated.

"Please, Sujay. It would be embarrassing. I had a rough day. Some friends were in trouble. It bought back some sad memories."

Sujay listened. He was 15. He understood the social implications. Absently, he reached down to pet Marshall, then he handed Al the paper. "I'm sorry," he said. "Um. Is everything okay now?"

"I don't know," Al said.

Sujay bit his lip and nodded. Because for God's sake men only nod. Men and near-men.

"Okay, well, I hope it all works out," Sujay said.

"Thank you," Al said. "I do, too."

Sujay hopped down the porch steps, grabbed his bike, and headed off.

A bike? Al thought for the first time. *How long is his route?*

Anil had come by one night, after the news had made its way. Anil had come by and offered his condolences and a bear hug, then slipped away quietly. The hug had shocked Al. It was born of an Anil he hadn't known. He had watched this small, slip of a man work his way back up the block between the intermittent street lights, in his Goodwill clothes and second hand shoes. Al had not thought his heart could hurt more right then, but watching Anil make his way home was somehow shattering.

Now as he watched Sujay cycle all the way down the long block and turn the corner onto 15th, Al realized that Sujay was a lot like his father. He understood dignity. Or maybe he understood fragility, Al wasn't sure.

Something in Sujay's kindness and then gentle departure had given Al, for the first time aside from the holidays, a sense of calm, even faith. A small, butterfly-winged hope. Fragile, easily torn. But there.

SARAH HAD CALLED sometime in the night, leaving a message. She had called again later, no message. Al didn't want to call her. His head felt full of air. He gave Marshall a head rub and some extra breakfast, showered, drank some strong coffee, and dressed for work. He crammed that new Macmillan textbook into his briefcase. The book weighed a ton. On his way out the door, he made certain to stop at Norda and Howard's and to put the newspaper in the door with his cell phone number scribbled on an attached note. As an afterthought, he added Glennie's number again. He had no idea what the hospital protocols were.

When he arrived at his office, he must have looked off balance because the department secretary brought him the last Danish from the staff room. He thanked her and rather than launch into any unsolicited commentary or confession, simply smiled and reached for his phone, though he had no one to call. Finally, he decided he'd better call Sarah. To his relief, she didn't pick up. He left a message, then he took a deep breath. He wanted to be alone. He needed time to re-establish the whole of himself. "It never leaves," he thought. "The grief never leaves. You just have to learn how to carry it."

Al opened his email to a reminder about a departmental meeting at 10. He spent most of the meeting checking his cell phone, and when it rang, he jumped up and hurried out, muttering apologies about urgent personal business. Al had expected Sarah. It was Glennie.

"There are HIPPA rules," she said, without preamble.

"I didn't ask anything," Al said.

Glennie paused. "Call your friend," she said.

"Can you tell me if it's bad news?"

But Glennie had already hung up.

Al left then. He drove home, to the peace of a quiet morning in a neighborhood in which the houses carried a hint of personality even without the noise that people bring. Homes painted different colors, lawns mannered but not immaculate. The occasional bike visible, the odd, vibrant, defiant weed. It was quiet enough now that one could hear the bees in the flowers. For a moment, Al paused in front of Norda and Howard's door. "What will you say when they tell you whatever it is they tell you?" Al thought, and then, "Who am I now?" He knew and knocked on the door.

When Sarah finally called later that night, Al grabbed the phone.

"Where are you?" he asked. "Are you okay?"

It was a gleeful Amelia who took the call, giggling, unable to adequately convey information. They were in Colorado, about to cross the state line into New Mexico. They were almost there.

Amelia wouldn't relinquish the phone, and Al said, "I love you, and tell Mommy I love her."

His voice sounded worn. He wondered if Amelia could tell.

Al wanted to speak with Sarah about his own journey, across the street. About how he had come to understand that his grief would be there, always. That afternoon, though, he had found a small place inside himself to tuck away his pain so that he could hear Norda and Howard's news, that this little baby was fine, that Norda needed to slow down. She couldn't be a hostess. He wanted to tell Sarah about holding Norda's bony, veined hand. He wanted to tell Sarah that he now understood some of his last thoughts in life would be of the child they had lost, and that at the very end he would be reaching out with some extension of his heart. And that maybe, maybe, there might be someone out there, up there, reaching back.

Amelia was chattering now. About restaurants and ice cream, about steering the car on a rutted back road, about how Mommy looked in her bandana. Alive, like electricity, his beautiful, beautiful girls.

Acknowledgments

All my heart and thanks to my family, which despite what these stories might suggest, is indeed a happy crew. Thank you to Rick, my rock, and my children, Colin and Alexandra, who always cheer me on. Thank you to Donna and David Hamilton for encouraging my writing from an early age, for reading drafts, and for giving me my first tiny dictionary—"because words are not enough." Thank you also to David and Trish Hamilton, for unflagging support.

A special thank you to Steve Yarbrough, Peter Geye, Hans Weyandt, Joni Rodgers and Linda Kass for their amazingly kind words about this collection.

Thank you to my friend, Dave Fox, for encouraging me to chase my dreams. It has been many years since that sushi dinner when you urged me to get cracking, but I never forgot and have appreciated your continued support in the years hence.

Thank you also to Dan Wickett, Erik Simon, Cary Johnson, Elisa Morris, Nancy Carpenter, Carl Lennertz, Kim Lara, April Eberhardt, Ann Weisgarber, Kathy Malik and Sara Speth—dear friends all whose encouragement for my writing as a whole helped me to keep going.

Thank you to *The Mud Season Review, Beloit Fiction Journal, Emerging Writers Network, Wisconsin Review, Long Story, Short, Puerto del Sol, Belmont Story Review* and *Hypertext Magazine* for first publishing or sharing my work.

Thank you to the Colorado State University MFA program staff, where many of these stories were first written, for a fantastic three years: David Milofsky, John Clark Pratt, Leslee Becker, and Steven Schwartz.

And a heartfelt thank you to Marc Estrin and Donna Bister for believing in me and in my stories and for shepherding me through the publication process with such wisdom and grace.

ABOUT THE AUTHOR

Caitlin Hamilton Summie earned an MFA with Distinction from Colorado State University, and her short stories have been published in Beloit Fiction Journal, Wisconsin Review, Puerto del Sol, Mud Season Review, and Long Story, Short. She spent many years in Massachusetts, Minnesota, and Colorado before settling with her family in Knoxville, Tennessee. She co-owns the book marketing firm, Caitlin Hamilton Marketing & Publicity, founded in 2003.

Fomite

About Fomite

A fomite is a medium capable of transmitting infectious organisms from one individual to another.

"The activity of art is based on the capacity of people to be infected by the feelings of others." Tolstoy, *What Is Art?*

Writing a review on Amazon, Good Reads, Shelfari, Library Thing or other social media sites for readers will help the progress of independent publishing. To submit a review, go to the book page on any of the sites and follow the links for reviews. Books from independent presses rely on reader to reader communications.

For more information or to order any of our books, visit http://www.fomitepress.com/FOMITE/Our_Books.html

More Titles from Fomite...

Novels

Joshua Amses — *During This, Our Nadir*
Joshua Amses — *Raven or Crow*
Joshua Amses — *The Moment Before an Injury*
Jaysinh Birjepatel — *The Good Muslim of Jackson Heights*
Jaysinh Birjepatel — *Nothing Beside Remains*
David Brizer — *Victor Rand*
Paula Closson Buck — *Summer on the Cold War Planet*
Marc Estrin — *Hyde*
Marc Estrin — *Speckled Vanitie*
Zdravka Evtimova — *Sinfonia Bulgarica*
Daniel Forbes — *Derail This Train Wreck*
Greg Guma — *Dons of Time*
Richard Hawley — *The Three Lives of Jonathan Force*

Fomite

Lamar Herrin — *Father Figure*
Ron Jacobs — *All the Sinners Saints*
Ron Jacobs — *Short Order Frame Up*
Ron Jacobs — *The Co-conspirator's Tale*
Scott Archer Jones — *A Rising Tide of People Swept Away*
Maggie Kast — *A Free Unsullied Land*
Darrell Kastin — *Shadowboxing with Bukowski*
Coleen Kearon — *Feminist on Fire*
Jan Englis Leary — *Thicker Than Blood*
Diane Lefer — *Confessions of a Carnivore*
Rob Lenihan — *Born Speaking Lies*
Ilan Mochari — *Zinsky the Obscure*
Gregory Papadoyiannis — *The Baby Jazz*
Andy Potok — *My Father's Keeper*
Robert Rosenberg — *Isles of the Blind*
Fred Skolnik — *Rafi's World*
Lynn Sloan — *Principles of Navigation*
L.E. Smith — *The Consequence of Gesture*
L.E. Smith — *Travers' Inferno*
Bob Sommer — *A Great Fullness*
Tom Walker — *A Day in the Life*
Susan V. Weiss —*My God, What Have We Done?*
Peter M. Wheelwright — *As It Is On Earth*
Suzie Wizowaty — *The Return of Jason Green*

Poetry
Antonello Borra — *Alfabestiario*
Antonello Borra — *AlphaBetaBestiaro*
James Connolly — *Picking Up the Bodies*
Greg Delanty — *Loosestrife*
Mason Drukman — *Drawing on Life*
J. C. Ellefson — *Foreign Tales of Exemplum and Woe*
Anna Faktorovich — *Improvisational Arguments*

Fomite

Stories

Fomite

Marjorie Maddox — *What She Was Saying*
William Marquess — *Boom-shacka-lacka*
Gary Miller — *Museum of the Americas*
Jennifer Anne Moses — *Visiting Hours*
Martin Ott — *Interrogations*
Jack Pulaski — *Love's Labours*
Charles Rafferty — *Saturday Night at Magellan's*
Kathryn Roberts — *Companion Plants*
Ron Savage — *What We Do For Love*
L.E. Smith — *Views Cost Extra*
Susan Thomas — *Among Angelic Orders*
Tom Walker — *Signed Confessions*
Silas Dent Zobal — *The Inconvenience of the Wings*

Odd Birds

Micheal Breiner — *the way none of this happened*
David Ross Gunn — *Cautionary Chronicles*
Gail Holst-Warhaft — *The Fall of Athens*
Roger Leboitz — *A Guide to the Western Slopes and the Outlying Area*
dug Nap— *Artsy Fartsy*
Delia Bell Robinson — *A Shirtwaist Story*
Peter Schumann — *Planet Kasper, Volumes One and Two*
Peter Schumann — *Bread & Sentences*
Peter Schumann — *Faust 3*
Peter Schumann — *We*

Plays

Stephen Goldberg — *Screwed and Other Plays*
Michele Markarian — *Unborn Children of America*

Made in the USA
Middletown, DE
26 November 2019